Maya Blake's hopes of becoming a writer were born when she picked up her first romance at thirteen. Little did she know her dream would come true! Does she still pinch herself every now and then to make sure it's not a dream? Yes, she does! Feel free to pinch her, too, via Twitter, Facebook or Goodreads! Happy reading!

Also by Maya Blake

The Sicilian's Banished Bride
The Commanding Italian's Challenge
The Greek's Hidden Vows
Reclaimed for His Royal Bed

Passion in Paradise

Kidnapped for His Royal Heir

The Notorious Greek Billionaires

Claiming My Hidden Son
Bound by My Scandalous Pregnancy

Discover more at millsandboon.co.uk.

BOUND BY HER RIVAL'S BABY

MAYA BLAKE

MILLS & BOON

First published in Great Britain 2022
by Mills & Boon, an imprint of HarperCollins*Publishers* Ltd,
1 London Bridge Street, London, SE1 9GF

www.harpercollins.co.uk

HarperCollins*Publishers*
1st Floor, Watermarque Building,
Ringsend Road, Dublin 4, Ireland

Large Print edition 2022

Bound by Her Rival's Baby © 2022 Maya Blake

ISBN: 978-0-263-29532-0

06/22

To Naana, my darling big sister.
This one, too, is for you, because
over forty books later,
without those first Mills & Boon
books you let me borrow,
I wouldn't be living this dream.

CHAPTER ONE

'EXCUSE ME, SIR. Your eleven o'clock appointment is here.'

Atu Quayson looked up from the blueprint he'd been scrutinising, his eyes narrowing on the personal assistant quivering in his office doorway.

He was going to have to replace her. She was far too timid, too skittish to withstand the brutally demanding work environment he excelled in.

He was a driven man and a taxing boss.

Some called him impossible. Others labelled him an arrogant brute to work for. Maybe there was truth to it. Atu simply saw himself as the direct product of his upbringing and made no excuses for it.

Why, then, had he allowed his mother to talk him into hiring her? His lips twisted. Yes…a friend of a friend of a friend's daughter, whose many professional qualities had been lauded, only for him to discover differently within a day of her installation in his office.

He stopped himself from gritting his teeth.

Perhaps, as his mother had archly suggested, the problem was him. And, while he would never admit it to her, he was beginning to entertain the possibility that she was right. That his bitter and austere view on life was bleeding onto his hapless subordinates.

But that was a problem to be tackled later.

'I don't have an eleven o'clock appointment.'

His tone didn't invite testing or defiance. He'd learned early in his professional life to memorise his daily schedule in case he needed to be flexible when new opportunities—or extraneous instances like his mother's interference—arose. He'd specifically cleared his diary until midday, when he met with his team of architects as he did every other Wednesday. A quick glance at his wristwatch confirmed that meeting was still an hour away.

Julie's—or was it Janet's?—eyes widened. 'Oh... um... I'm sorry, sir, but she's very adamant that you see her.'

His hackles rose higher. 'She?' Suspicion of his mother's hand in this too swirled acid through his gut. On top of everything else, he didn't need the once-a-month, stay-out-of-my-business verbal skirmish with his mother, a battle he usually fooled himself into thinking he'd won, only to discover she'd merely retreated to plot her next move.

'Did this person give you a name or a reason

why she feels entitled to see me?' He made no effort to hide his disgruntlement.

Her fingers twitched a few times, then went into full-on hand-wringing. 'She said you would know what it was about. And her name is...' She stopped and cleared her throat, patently terrified to utter the name. 'Her name is Amelie Hayford, sir.'

Atu jerked upright, the unpleasant sensation in his gut thickening until his whole being was immersed in a soup of acid. Immersed in memories he didn't like to recall today or ever.

His heart slammed against his ribs, each beat echoing the surname no one in his family willingly spoke aloud. Not unless it was absolutely necessary. Unless it was a reminder to stay the course.

For the sake of vengeance.

For the sake of stoking the fires of retribution that kept his father alive even now, on what doctors whispered was his deathbed.

'What did you say?' His voice was an unsheathed blade and real apprehension shifted in the PA's eyes.

She cast a furtive glance over her shoulder, then whispered, 'A-Amelie... Hayford, sir,' as if lowering the decibels of her response would minimise its impact.

It didn't. Her confirmation merely increased the roiling inside him, shaking loose several pertinent questions.

Would she really dare?

Why hadn't she been stopped by Security at the entrance to his building?

How had she made it all the way to his penthouse office?

He operated from the top floor of his flagship Quayson Group hotel, located in the centre of Accra, for a reason—so casual acquaintances, unwanted guests and sycophants couldn't drop in at will. It was also why his security was top-notch.

His fingers started to clench but he wilfully stopped himself from tensing. Displaying the sort of emotion that bubbled underneath his skin was no longer useful.

Emotion had torn his family apart. Twisted obsession and forbidden love had ripped through it, the disease infesting everything he treasured, leaving devastation in its wake and him with the searing belief that control, emotional austerity and dedication to professional goals were the only things that would sustain him.

So he inhaled deeply and returned his gaze to the blueprints spread out on his table. 'Inform her that an appointment with me or anyone in my company needs to be assessed and agreed upon. Without exception. I'm not some fast-food drive-through she can swing past when the urge takes her.'

'Perhaps you'd like to say that to my face?' came a husky voice, making his PA jump.

Atu's head snapped to the doorway a second before the owner of the voice came into view.

With a confidence he would have admired, had he not been caught in the vortex of memory, bitterness and, yes, *shame*, the tall, voluptuous woman swept past the distraught PA and entered his domain.

As if she had every right.

As if she was intent on proving she wasn't still the timid child he'd grown up with, who'd lurked on the fringes of his close-knit friends and family group back when their families had been the closest of friends, instead of the vicious enemies they were now.

But hadn't he had a taste of the confident, defiant woman even back then? Hadn't she effortlessly punched through the brittle shell of anger and bitterness he'd built around himself that night eight years ago when, fresh from yet *another* row with his father, he'd crossed paths with her? Even then she'd sent him reeling hard, triggering an awareness that underneath her wide-eyed innocence a vibrant, passionate and confident woman lurked. One who'd burrowed beneath his guard... tempted him into a torrid episode that plagued him in imprudent moments.

Like now.

She moved towards him as if she owned the very air he breathed. And perhaps, on some level, she did. Because he was suddenly finding it difficult to take a breath, the captivating effect of her presence capsizing the smooth mechanics of his respiratory system.

He saw his PA reaching for the door to shut it, hurriedly making herself scarce, but his attention was wholly locked on the woman before him.

He ignored her question, attempting to catalogue the components of her that made up this curiously intriguing, highly unwanted package.

Faint gold and orange eyeshadow highlighted her big, beautiful eyes and flawless face. A face framed by the yellow and green patchwork making up her high kente headdress and the tasteful gold hoop earrings dangling from her lobes. Her chunky colourful necklace invited the gaze to the regal grace of her slim neck, sloping onto elegant shoulders, currently bare save for the thin straps holding up the knee-length bright yellow dress moulded to her body. Long, shapely legs tapered down to feet adorned with stylish gold heels.

She was a woman who knew which colours did her justice, and she'd chosen well today.

Advancing further, she extended one graceful arm, set down her handbag before bracing her hands on her hips. She cocked one eyebrow in challenge.

She'd come prepared for battle. Her suit of armour was her confidence. Her unflinching pride. The intelligence shining in her eyes. Perhaps even her stunning beauty. Although the first three would have cowed a less formidable man, the fourth was the thing that clinched a victory.

He wasn't cowed. Because he couldn't forget for one second what this woman and the blood that ran through her veins embodied.

The destruction of his family.

He folded his arms, resisting the urge to rake his gaze over her once more. To linger on those plump lips he'd tasted once eight years ago, in a moment of madness that still haunted him.

He might have abandoned the pursuit of the opposite sex for a while, to concentrate on his current project, and to save himself the trouble of his mother's rabid matchmaking every time he so much as glanced at a woman. But he didn't welcome his suddenly raging libido reminding him of that fact now. Especially not with this woman.

'You're brave. I'll give you that. Arguably, foolish too. Either way, I recommend you turn around and use that door behind you while you have the chance.'

Her chin angled up higher, her stare growing bolder. 'Or what?'

He cocked his brow in return. 'Surely you can't be that dense? We may not have seen each other in eight years, but surely you haven't forgotten the circumstances of our last meeting?'

That harrowing day when two beloved people had been laid to rest, ironically and unfortunately in side-by-side burial crypts neither family had wanted to relinquish even in the face of their searing grief and loss.

Atu darkly mused what would be etched on their tombstones several lifetimes from now—the Quaysons and the Hayfords, two families who had vowed never to back down in destroying each other, even in death.

Shades of distress moved in her eyes, then disappeared in the next second. Atu wasn't sure whether to admire her strength of will or add it to the grievance list carved into his family's soul.

'I'm not here to rehash the past with you. Your actions left me with no choice but to come here. Or are you going to claim equal denseness?'

He shifted as her voice washed over him. She spoke in the accented Ghanaian English he would be able to pick out in a sea of a thousand voices anywhere in the world. Throughout his long absences from his motherland, hearing the distinct accent had triggered a sense of home and comfort he experienced whenever he heard it.

But added to Amelie's accent were British overtones—the result of having spent half her life studying and living in London.

His own speech was laced with the influences of a childhood spent in the States and then around the world, living the carefree life of the 'spare' while his much-beloved older brother revelled in being the heir.

Until it had all crashed to a bleak and devastating halt.

The reminder dragged him from his musings. 'What do you want, Miss Hayford?'

She tensed, most likely in reaction to his formal address.

Their last interaction that fateful weekend eight

years ago had started off as a terse conversation, riddled with mild threats and spiked accusations, mostly fuelled by one too many cocktails.

And then it had turned into something else. Something he preferred to forget. But not even then had he been this formal.

Again, she got her emotions under control rapidly.

Reaching into her bag, she retrieved a sheaf of papers. 'My lawyers have informed you of my refusal to sell my resort to you on numerous occasions, *Mr Hayford*. And yet *this* arrived this morning.'

He allowed mockery to seep into his features and his voice. 'I'm aware of what my lawyers are doing on my behalf. What's your point?'

She slapped the documents on his desk. 'Since I can only conclude that there's been a break in communication, I've decided to tell you face to face. *I'm not interested.*'

'Don't the phones work in your backward resort? A shame you had to leave your little hamlet. Or have you moved back to the city?'

He knew the answer to that.

She lived near Saltpond, a thriving coastal city two hours west of Accra, while he resided in the capital. Accra was a rich and vibrantly diverse city, but it was also a relatively small city, made even smaller when one existed within the elite social circles he and his family inhabited. The same circles her family used to enjoy.

And when those two families were inextricably linked by personal tragedy, it was impossible not to be aware of one another. If she hadn't come straight here, he would've known by lunchtime that she was in town. Unfailingly, his mother would have made it her business to inform him and every member of the family that a Hayford was back in her beloved city.

'I'm not going to dignify your pathetic insults with a response,' she said, shoving the documents at him before pivoting away from him, her hands clenched into fists.

Her movement highlighted her proud breasts and curvy hips, contrasted by her tiny waist, currently cinched in by a wide tanned leather belt bearing the hallmarks of the talents of the Northern Region of their homeland. Heat punched into him as he watched her, unable to drag his gaze from a body that was a siren song he was sure must draw most men.

Most men.

Not him.

He mentally doused the flames invading his

groin, summoning the iron-forged willpower that had helped him withstand his father's merciless censure for his part in their family tragedy and its ongoing dysfunction. The same dogged control that kept the vault of his guilt and regret intact.

To him, Amelie could only be an ornament that caught the corner of his eye. Intriguing for a vague little second, but forgotten about once he'd achieved his latest goal—acquiring the comparatively small Hayford Beach Resort and absorbing it into the latest Quayson Group project.

He refused to allow himself to dwell on those moments when he'd lost himself in the feel and taste of her, blindly and desperately seeking to forget the forceful demands of his father, the stark reminder that he would always be second-best. That he existed solely to be the wind beneath his more deserving brother's wings.

Just as he refused to accommodate the twinge of regret about giving in to his weakness with Amelie that night.

Because she'd been using him too...

All that mattered was the present. Pursuing his goal without the distraction she represented was why he kept his dealings strictly between their lawyers.

Her pacing brought her close once more, and

he saw the moment she spotted the draft blue-prints he'd been reviewing. Faint apprehension flickered over her face before being eradicated by utter derision.

'You've had blueprints done on *my* resort? You're getting a little bit ahead of yourself, aren't you?' she taunted.

'Not at all. In fact, my team is running a little bit behind schedule.'

Chocolate-brown eyes rose to his, anger sparking in the depths. Against the brown, the stark white of her eyes stood out sharply, highlighting her glorious mocha skin. It was several shades lighter than his own dark mahogany hue, and whatever make-up she'd applied made it gleam in the sunlight slanting through his windows.

Hell, she glowed with a vitality that made his fingers itch to explore her. He was sure this kind of radiance was reserved for some goddess. The kind that caused men to lose their minds. The kind of power her own sister had wielded against his brother. And look how that had ended.

Tragedy, devastation and the rabid quest for vengeance.

'Oh, and you can call off your spy,' she added with a snap. 'I know you conned my deputy manager into spilling company secrets. His employment has been terminated. And, just so we're clear, my resort isn't for sale now or in the fore-seeable future.'

'Then why did you meet with investors from Dubai last month?'

Stunned surprise flickered in her eyes but her chin rose higher. 'That's no one's business—especially not yours or your deplorable family's.'

Fury sparked in his gut. While he had his own issues with his family, an inexplicable vein of loyalty had kept him anchored to them even as he'd enjoyed his hard-won freedom on the other side of the globe. That loyalty remained alive and well.

'Watch your tone,' he growled, all mockery wiped from his voice.

She didn't back down. 'What are you going to do? Have your security throw me out? I'll remind you that you're not the only one with connec-tions. You currently have several deals in delicate stages. Think how it'll look if you're embroiled in a scandal. And, trust me, anything but a seem-ingly cordial meeting between us will make it onto social media within the hour. Are you will-ing to risk adverse publicity and displease your business partners?'

Her threats ignited a different fire inside him.

He'd always relished a challenge, and even this brief skirmish—and he intended it to be brief, because every second in her presence reminded him of those forbidden minutes when they'd tangled together—roused the spirit of the Fante warriors who'd sired his bloodline and hers.

'I won't need my security to help me throw you out. I'll urge you to recall our family history. Remember how the Hayfords have fared against the Quaysons so far and consider the likelihood of you coming out on top of whatever scheme you're proposing.'

Her throat moved in a delicate swallow, but her gaze remained defiant. 'And that's a source of pride for you, is it?' she jeered, her nose very much in the air.

He recalled then that, while his family could boast an impressive pedigree, Amelie Hayford's progenitors were actual royalty. And with every flash of her eyes and haughty proclamation, the echoes of her regal forebears shone through.

Not that it mattered one iota in this time and place, he assured himself sternly. Her sister's emotional manipulation of his brother was partly the reason Fiifi was no longer alive. The reason his father was steeped in bitterness and his family irreversibly set on vengeance. Because some-one had to pay, didn't they?

It was why he'd returned to the family fold after years of being labelled the black sheep—a title he'd nonchalantly shrugged on, another layer to add to the many denigrating layers his father had seen fit to saddle him with.

As for Amelie herself—perhaps if he hadn't let his base instincts take over that night, he would've been able to stop…

Enough!

This meeting had run long enough. As had the unsettling memory-dredging. 'It's time for you to leave. And I'd advise against talking to the press or making any precipitate moves against me or my company.'

Her eyes flashed. 'Tell me you'll stop sniffing around my business and you won't need to see or hear from me for the remainder of your de-spicable life.'

For some absurd reason, the thought of never seeing her again chafed—as if he'd brushed up against sandpaper in the dark. 'I'll have to disappoint you. Your little resort falls into my expansion objectives. Whether you make my ac-quisition of it hostile or civil is entirely up to you.'

'*Civil?*' She spat the word as if it was poison. 'You don't know the meaning of the word.'

He bit his tongue against reminding her that things between them hadn't always been hostile. That for a handful of minutes one memorable night she'd melted in his arms. She'd moaned his name and pressed her alluring body against his.

He clenched his gut against the unwelcome reminder. 'Really? What do you call showing up unannounced in my office, throwing down ultimatums?'

'You left me no choice. Stop coming after what's mine and I won't make any unannounced visits. Your actions are drawing unwanted attention and I won't have that.'

His eyes narrowed. 'What kind of attention?' he breathed.

He'd seen off the Dubai delegations, easily interesting them in his much more lucrative projects in Cape Town and Malaysia. Just as he'd seen off the Lebanese conglomerate and the US one before that.

Even without his father's zealous interest in acquiring the small resort on the beautiful southern coast of Ghana—simply because it was a Hayford property and, after a decade-long endeavour, the last meaningful Hayford holding and therefore the final thing standing in the way of the Quaysons accomplishing their revenge—Atu's own assessment of the resort and, more importantly, its potential had sparked an interest he'd been unable to ignore.

If he could achieve both his aims in one go, all the better.

'That's none of your concern,' she snapped, reclaiming his attention.

Her breathing had grown shallower with her agitation, dragging his focus to the pulse racing at her throat. To the impressive swell of her breasts and the rich, enthralling scent of her perfume. That maddeningly intoxicating mixture of shea butter and coconut that pulsed from her skin.

An image lit up in his head, of him burying his face in the curve of her neck, inhaling her scent while stifling a groan. Then gliding his tongue over that speeding pulse, being rewarded with her hitched breathing. Just like he'd done that night.

Awuradzi Yesu.

Thankful the curse hadn't slipped free of his control the way his thoughts were running rampant, he turned away from her, pinching the bridge of his nose when she continued speaking.

'There are literally miles of beachfront properties along the south coast. Why are you obsessed with mine?'

He faced her again, attempting not to fixate on the plumpness of the mouth that had spoken the words. 'You're in a prime location, with rich tourism within shouting distance. It's also an easy trek from Accra. I'd be a fool to overlook it.'

Her nostrils flared in anger. 'So you'll take it by force?'

For the briefest second, he experienced a pang of something eerily close to guilt. Then he shook himself free of it. 'Hardly. My lawyers have made you several very generous offers.'

'All of which I've turned down. Doesn't that tell you something?'

'It tells me you're stubborn. It also tells me you're in danger of finding yourself out of your depth if you cling to that stubbornness.'

'What's that supposed to mean?'

He allowed himself a small smile. 'You really think I'm going to lay all my cards on the table?'

Again, she easily smothered any trepidation she might feel. 'I have the blessing of the chief. Saltpond runs in my blood. Local support alone will ensure you lose any takeover bid.'

'You might have his ear, but what I offer will

be far greater than any advantage born out of clansmanship.'

'And what's that?'

Atu decided it wouldn't hurt to demonstrate a fraction of the clout he wielded. 'Your resort employs how many? Sixty? Eighty?'

Her eyes narrowed. 'Ninety-five,' she bit out.

He stopped himself from smirking in triumph. Deep down, he hadn't wanted this task. Hadn't wanted to be here in Accra at all. He'd been perfectly happy in Malaysia, far away from the bitterness and the zealous family vendetta and politics. He had been fine leaving the running of the questionable family empire to his father.

In his resort on the Desaru Coast, he didn't have to see the cruelty-tinted grief etched into his father's face, the not-so-secret light in his parent's eyes that told him he wished things had turned out differently that night.

That perhaps even the wrong son had been taken...

Better still, there he wasn't reminded daily of his own disagreement with his father that day which had blinded him to everything else. Of the fact that if he'd focused his attention outwardly, instead of dwelling on the dejection churning in his chest, he would have noticed Fiifi was drinking too much. That the woman his older brother had purported to desire above all else had an agenda of her own…

He shook himself free of the grappling hooks of the past and laid down the bare facts for the woman standing before him.

'When I take over your resort and implement my expansion plans, I'll generate over three hundred jobs. I'll elevate the whole area and create healthy competition with the resorts in Cape Coast and Takoradi. Do you truly believe your chief will pass up such an opportunity?'

Doubt crept into her eyes and lingered for several seconds before she dismissed his words. 'He'll see through all that to the truth—that you're just in it for the profit.'

His eyebrows spiked. 'And you're not? Are you running a charity?'

'I provide a personalised experience, tailor-made for every guest. I'm not a faceless corporate giant that simply offers a place to lay your head for the night and charges a fortune for it.'

'You haven't done your homework properly if you believe the Quayson Group is just another run-of-the-mill chain hotelier.'

Her lips pursed. 'Stuff your corporate spiel. And stop trying to paint yourself as some altruistic businessman with the best interests of the ordinary man at heart. I've first-hand knowledge of the kind of man you are, remember?'

The force of their history ploughed through the space between them. For a single raw moment their combined grief and loss thickened in the air.

Then she pivoted and sashayed to where she'd dropped her bag.

He would have had to be dead from the neck down to stop his gaze from sliding down to her round, firm buttocks and her supple hips.

His mouth dried and he bit back a curse. He had a weakness for voluptuous women, and while, at twenty, Amelie Hayford had retained some aspects of girlishness, at twenty-eight she was all woman, with an hourglass figure that reminded him he was profoundly male and at risk of announcing that he was aroused by the very epitome of the goddess now taking command of his office.

'I thought you weren't here to dredge up history?' he replied, with more bite than he'd intended. 'But if you're in the mood for that, I can remind you of another time you played out of your league.'

She tensed, then sent him a searing glance over her shoulder. 'I have no idea what you're talking about,' she said a little too hurriedly. Too breath-lessly.

Again, her chest rose and fell with her breath-ing, stirring his blood a little too fast.

She riled him.

Every Hayford riled him and his family in some way. But since that night when he'd let his emo-tions get the better of him, Amelie had been able to burrow deep under his skin, as if she had spe-cial dispensation from the gods to add an extra layer of hell, fashioned just for him.

He wasn't desperate to examine that particular layer—wasn't sure he wanted to discover what the unwanted ingredient was.

He especially wasn't interested in discovering if it was anything like what his brother had suf-fered from. Some had labelled it weakness. Oth-ers had called it obsession. Whatever it had been, it had driven Fiifi over the edge.

He, Atu, was above that. Had striven to keep himself from that kind of unnecessary entangle-ment. He wasn't about to start now.

'Count yourself lucky I don't have the time or inclination to refresh your memory.'

For a handful of seconds her eyes widened, her lips parting in a single breath. Then she faced him fully, spearing him with a fierce look from far too enchanting eyes. 'Luck has nothing to do with it. I'll just keep reminding myself that *okoto nwo anoma*. Isn't that how the saying goes?'

He tossed the proverb in his head, striving to maintain his cool. *A crab doesn't birth a bird.* Meaning he was culpable in whatever sins she laid at his family's feet.

'Again, while I'd love to compare notes on which one of us bears the most blame in our little family drama, I'm afraid I'll have to pass. I have a meeting in five minutes.'

Her eyes narrowed. 'Don't try me, Atu. I'm warning you.'

His name on her lips caused a deep rumbling inside him, like a shift of the tectonic plates that formed his existence. It pooled in latent heat in his groin and slowly intensified as they faced off.

In that moment, he realised that, no, he didn't resent this project thrust upon him as much as he should. Perhaps, subconsciously, he even relished it. Because, for good or ill, he wasn't going to let this go.

Hell, maybe this would be the purge that drove the dark shadows from his life.

The final slice of retribution for his family.

Especially for the brother he'd let down.

Maybe then he'd be free of the guilt and shame.

Maybe then his father would even look at him without rancour from the cold embrace of his deathbed.

Whatever the reason behind it, the spark had ignited in him, and now grew to a burning flame of purpose.

He was going to conquer this thorn in his family's side once and for all.

And by coming here, Amelie Hayford had put herself in the centre of his war of redemption.

CHAPTER TWO

AMELIE WANTED TO scream in frustration—and, yes, also release the knot of trepidation in her gut—when the courier delivered the now familiar richly embossed white envelope with the well-known law firm's logo etched into the top right-hand corner.

For five days she'd fooled herself into thinking her actions had reaped the desired result.

She'd braved the lion's den and barely escaped with her emotions intact. So what if she'd been unable to stop the angry frustration and never-ending grief she carried from filtering through in unguarded moments?

Altogether, it had gone better than she'd hoped. She'd delivered her message. The big, bad corporate giant intending to invade her sanctuary would heed her warning and back off.

The old enemies her family had deliberately distanced themselves from by moving a few hundred miles would stay in their place and in the past.

How foolishly hopeful had she been?

'Don't try me, Atu. I'm warning you.'

That last volley, scrambled together after his

pointed declaration that he couldn't even be bothered to dredge up those scorching, illicit moments they'd shared, had merely earned her stare and then a humourless, teeth-baring smile resembling a predator indulging in a weak prey's antics.

She'd known it was time to beat a hasty retreat.

Nevertheless, she'd been proud of not backing down.

Now she knew it had all been for nothing.

In typical Quayson fashion, he'd blithely ignored her, intent on taking what he wanted, regardless of who stood in his way. Regardless of the pain he caused.

With the delivery of yet another offer—sweetened with a further several hundred thousand dollars, as if money would sway her—it was clear Atu Quayson was still set on acquiring her resort.

She chewed worriedly on her bottom lip.

Her options were rapidly dwindling. Despite her bravado in Atu's office, the resort was struggling.

September was fast approaching, and with it the end of the peak and most lucrative season. In a little over a month she would be down to less than half-capacity, with even fewer guests until the Christmas period brought a seasonal end-of-year injection of cash. Cash she very much needed to make vital repairs, maintain general upkeep, and to fight whatever hostile takeover Atu Quayson planned.

But that injection would only be a few weeks' worth. She'd kept repairs and plans to hire new staff on ice, but sooner or later she'd need to undertake both if she was to keep up with the level of excellence she'd boasted about.

There was also the small matter of the refurbishment loan she hadn't known existed until after her father had passed away and she'd seen the true state of the resort's books. A loan she was still paying off and would continue to be saddled with for another five years. That was why she couldn't afford to let a single standard slip. Why she had to keep the serene swanlike glide for appearances' sake while pedalling furiously to keep afloat.

The cycle of just keeping her head above water wasn't going to hold for much longer. Especially when she was surrounded by sharks—the largest of which being her far too disturbing nemesis.

She'd tried to block out Atu's effect on her during their meeting. Tried to smother the memories of the night her sister and his brother had died.

But all it had taken was one look for her to remember her years-long stupid crush, the sultry nights she'd spent fighting off the fevered arousal he sparked inside her with a simple glance, the days she'd spent back then cursing her family for not settling their differences, for robbing her of what she'd so deeply craved—the attention of the most dynamic man she'd ever known.

The Quaysons and the Hayfords hadn't always been enemies.

On the contrary, the first twelve years of her childhood had been a blissful adventure of joint family holidays, weekends and birthdays spent in each other's adjoining homes, small and large milestone celebrations filled with joy and laughter, the promise of endless possibilities.

Naana Quayson, the matriarch of the Quayson clan, was her godmother, for heaven's sake. They couldn't have been closer, except by being related by blood, if they'd tried.

It had started to go wrong over a simple business disagreement the summer she'd turned thirteen. Even then the two families had tolerated each other for a few more years. But like a rolling stone gathering momentum, petty rivalries had grown, and their inability to settle their differences had eaten its way like acid through their families.

Throw in Joseph Quayson's growing power,

arrogance, and a series of risky but fruitful business ventures that had seen him gain financial leverage over her own equally proud, equally arrogant father, and the bonfire that would rip their families apart for ever had been lit.

That had been before personal tragedy had completely decimated them.

Joseph Quayson had lost his firstborn son and heir.

Amelie had lost her beloved sister.

She shook herself free from the memories. From the effect of what being in the same room as Atu after eight years had done to her equilibrium.

With one simple quirk of his eyebrow and a sweep of his arrogant gaze, he'd reminded her of their capricious history—especially the searing encounter that had catapulted her from girl to woman within a handful of heartbeats.

He'd reminded her that she was a woman with needs gone far too long unheeded and lately completely abandoned.

Her last two relationships had lacked the elusive spice and pit-of-the-stomach excitement she'd discovered she needed—missing ingredients that being in Atu's presence had effortlessly, annoyingly sparked.

Far too many times in his office she'd forgotten herself and made the mistake of entertaining the lustful need he'd evoked at their last encounter.

But she only needed to glance at her mother, see the faraway look in her eyes that said her thoughts were with Esi, her first child, to be brought back to earth. To remember that the memory of the sister she'd lost in the same crash that had killed Fiifi Quayson in that cruel and harrowing week of loss and tragedy eight years ago forbade her from ever thinking about their kiss.

That look arrived in her mother's eyes much too frequently these days and lingered for too long. It was a look Amelie had grappled with for a long time before accepting the hard truth—that for her mother she would never be as good as her sister's memory. Would never come close to filling the hole Esi had left in her mother's heart.

The fact that that, in turn, had left a hole in Amelie's heart wasn't a truth she liked to dwell on. Grief and wishful thoughts for a better relationship with her mother wouldn't keep a roof over their heads for long. Not if Atu remained hell-bent on acquiring her resort.

She set down the documents and clicked on her emails, rubbing her temples as she read the other buyout offers.

Now her treacherous deputy manager had been fired, she could keep this latest offer under her hat for a while, but inevitably Atu Quayson would get wind of it. He probably already knew that, as of today, his was the most lucrative offer. Just as *she* knew that even if he increased it by a thousand per cent she still wouldn't accept it.

Not without becoming a traitor to her family.

Not without breaking her mother's heart.

Amelie grimaced as memory broke the chain of her restraint again. Then she closed her eyes as she was propelled back to that night.

Fiifi, the Quayson heir, turning twenty-five had meant he'd been handed the much-anticipated keys to the kingdom.

The occasion had been marked by the party to end all parties. A party she and her family had been invited to, despite the mounting tensions crackling in the background like live wires. At the time, Amelie had been relieved when her parents had declined, and quietly ecstatic when Esi had insisted Amelie accompany her.

Fiifi had set his sights on her sister, and for all her strong-willed independence, Esi had fallen for him.

Amelie had kept her opinion that Fiifi was unsuitable for her older sister to herself—like the rest of the Quayson sons, he possessed far too many of his father's traits—purely because she'd wanted to go to the party for her own selfish reasons.

She'd wanted to be close to Atu.

So she'd dismissed the reason behind Esi's erratic behaviour, had turned a blind eye to the fact that beneath the wild gaiety her sister had looked desperately unhappy. That Fiifi had been equally worked up about...*something*.

Instead, she'd fixed all her attention on the second son brooding in the corner, glaring icily at anyone who ventured near.

It had taken two cocktails to bolster her confidence enough to approach him. To strike up an inane conversation that had turned those piercing dark eyes her way, then trapped her like hapless prey.

And when he'd silenced her with one long finger over her runaway mouth before leading her to an even quieter corner, she'd gone willingly, feverish anticipation firing up every cell in her body.

She'd happily ignored everything going on under her nose. By the time she'd come crashing back to earth, it had been too late.

The heart of her family had been torn out, shredded with pain and grief.

The family feud that had taken her sister had stolen her father too, four years later—although his demise had been slow and tortuous, coming by way of drinking himself into liver failure and eventual death.

This resort, despite its challenges, was the only substantial thing the family had been left with in the wake of years of feuding. Atu would get his hands on it over her dead body.

She looked up in relief as her manager, Maria, knocked and entered. 'You wanted to know when today's guests arrived? I've checked in a handful, but a few more have just turned up, including an…interesting one.'

Amelie nodded, gratefully putting her troubles aside for a while.

Greeting guests was technically Maria and her team's job, but Amelie loved knowing who was staying in her beautiful, quirky thatched chalets, and took delight in matching characters to the individually stylised suites and hearing positive feedback.

That attention to detail had earned her 'signature resort' status and glowing reviews—although not a boost in guest numbers. Nevertheless, she treasured those reviews as much as she treasured seeing her family name etched on the soaring wooden welcome arch at the resort's entrance.

The last thing she intended was to hand it over to the sterile, profit-orientated Quayson Group.

Her conscience stung with a flicker of shame as she rose from her desk. The Quayson Group resorts were spectacular. Luxurious to the point of decadence, with an eye-watering price tag to go with it, from what she'd seen online. And, yes, it seemed they had the same ferocious attention to detail she admired.

Still, this resort was hers and—

Her thoughts screeched to a halt, along with her feet, when she stepped out of her office and saw the man standing at the far side of the reception area.

It was as if she'd conjured him up by thought alone.

Atu Quayson was facing away from her, his gaze on the jaw-dropping sea view that made hers the hilltop promontory location everyone within a fifty-mile radius craved. And yet she recognised those broad shoulders and tapering torso, that strong masculine neck and chiselled jawline. He didn't need to turn for her to recall the impressive blade of his nose and wide, sensual mouth.

The sheen of his vibrant dark mahogany skin overlaying his sleek, well-toned male perfection.

His hair was close-cropped, the edges of his tight inky black curls neatly outlined by an expensive barber's clippers, perfectly delineating his face and compelling more than his fair share of gazes from the females who'd found reason to be in the reception area.

Amelie curbed a dart of jealous annoyance.

'How...when did he arrive?' she asked in a hushed tone, belatedly recalling Maria's allusion to their 'interesting' guest.

Amelie wished she'd paid more attention. Wished she'd had time to gird her loins, calm the erratic beat of her heart.

'About ten minutes ago,' Maria whispered back, wariness in her tone. 'He wasn't in a hurry to check in, which is why I came to get you.'

No, of course not. He was too busy eyeing up her business, seeking out its weak spots.

Like most of her employees, Maria knew the Quayson-Hayford history. It was right up there with local folklore, after all, she thought dryly.

'I don't remember seeing his name on the guest bookings.' She was one hundred per cent sure she'd have noticed.

Maria's lips pursed. 'Neither do I. But there's

a corporate booking which is probably his. The name didn't ring any bells. I'm sorry, Amelie.'

She touched the older woman's arm reassuringly. 'Don't be. You weren't to know.'

About to stalk over to him, she paused. 'Is my mother here?' she asked, panic flaring inside her. The last thing she needed was a confrontation between her mother and the black sheep of the Quayson family. Or any member of that family, for that matter.

Maria shook her head. 'She asked for lunch to be delivered to her at the residence.'

Amelie breathed a sigh of relief, although this was yet another sign of the changes in her mother, who'd taken to spending the majority of her time at the home they shared at the edge of the resort instead of coming for the daily lunches she'd used to take in the restaurant, just to keep an eye on things.

'Are you going to allow him to stay?'

Maria asked the question Amelie herself had tossed feverishly in her mind moments ago. To all intents and purposes Atu Quayson was a guest. Manufacturing a reason to reject his confirmed booking went against her principles.

She gritted her teeth. 'I don't think I have a choice.'

Maria nodded with a touch of sympathy and then, beckoned by the concierge, she excused herself.

Amelie stepped behind the reception desk, took her time to greet the new guests, while keeping a surreptitious eye on Atu.

She knew the moment he turned from the view because her skin heated up and the hairs on her nape tingled with deep awareness as he strode towards the desk, his gaze pinned on her.

The air thinned out, making breathing difficult. When she managed to snatch in a quietly desperate breath, it was to have her senses infused with the dark, earthy spice of his aftershave, coupled with a layer of male pheromones that caused her belly muscles to tremble.

'Good afternoon, Amelie.'

She wanted to demand that he not use her given name in that far too evocative way. That he stop leaning on her oak-hewn countertop, exposing his brawny forearms and powerful wrists, those capable hands and far too elegant fingers that made her want to relive his touch. *Again.*

No, she most definitely wasn't going to think about that.

Instead, she pinned a cool, professional smile on her face, forced the traitorous swarm of but-

terflies down. 'Mr Quayson, I'm sure there must
be some mistake. If you took a wrong turn, I'd
be happy to point you in the direction of where
you wish to go...'

That slow, predatory smile reappeared, and his
incisive gaze combed leisurely over her body before meeting hers. 'No need. I'm exactly where
I need to be.'

She tilted her head contemplatively, allowing
a musing smile to play at her lips, and immediately regretted it when his gaze zeroed in on her
mouth. 'Really?' she asked. 'Because I don't see
your name anywhere on today's reservations list.'

'I've already given your receptionist the name
the booking was made under. I'd be happy to re-
peat myself if necessary?' he offered, mockery
thick in his voice.

She quietly bristled at the faint insult, but managed to keep her smile in place. 'Any reason
why you felt the need to hide behind a corporate
name?'

He shrugged, drawing her attention to the insanely broad expanse of his shoulders. His were
the type of shoulders a woman fantasised about
clinging to in the depths of passion. Gripping
desperately to as she was swept away by bliss.

Objectively speaking, of course, she cautioned

herself. Because this particular exhibit of male perfection was strictly out of bounds.

'If I'd wished to infiltrate your little resort, I would've found a way to do it without your knowledge. I booked under a corporate name because my team knows I value my privacy. Speaking of which—perhaps we should get on with things, before my infamy gets the better of the situation?'

His droll voice made her glance around.

Sure enough, a smattering of onlookers were lurking, either anticipating fireworks or just keen to be in the revered orbit of a Quayson.

Beyond the fact that Atu Quayson's well-publicised rebellion against his father had earned him the 'black sheep' label long before he'd succeeded at building his own individual hotel empire, before returning to the family fold two years ago, the Quaysons' wealth and stature had already gained them revered status in Ghanaian society.

Acknowledgement from a Quayson was almost literally worth its weight in gold. Joseph Quayson was known to occasionally lavish gold nuggets from his private goldmine upon friends and loved ones in a show of extravagant generosity.

A goldmine which should've partly belonged to my father.

That searing reminder helped dissipate a few layers of Atu's effect on her, helping her focus as she straightened her spine. 'Of course,' she said crisply. 'A paying guest is a paying guest.'

With swift efficiency, she booked him in, choosing the most exclusive of her ten VIP chalets. Besides being one of the best chalets, it was also at the furthest end of the grounds, on a high cliff overlooking the sea. With any luck, he wouldn't need to encounter her mother any time soon.

Or at all, if she convinced him to leave…

She activated his key card, but he stopped her before she could summon a bellhop.

'That won't be necessary.' He lifted a sleek weekend bag, and she spotted the super-exclusive designer logo etched into the rich brown leather. 'This is all I have with me.'

Perhaps she should've been relieved he wasn't planning on a long stay, but all she felt was a greater wariness that he believed whatever he'd come here for would be achieved within a day or two.

His fingers brushed hers as he took the key card. She snatched her hand back, unwilling to endure another second of the fever that rushed through her system at his touch.

'What I would like is an escort to my room, though,' he drawled, in that deep, far too sexy baritone that sang along her nerves before burrowing into her secret places. 'Just in case I wander into places I'm not supposed to be.'

Knowing he'd read her thoughts made her skin tingle with even more awareness. 'You're here, in my resort, in the first place. Did you think about whether I'd want you here before you arrived?' She couldn't stem the bitterness in her voice.

He shrugged, a lazy stretch of muscles that said he didn't give a damn about her thoughts. That he wouldn't be moved by word or deed to do anything other than what he wanted. 'I'm hoping that by the time I leave here we'll both have something we want.'

She gritted her teeth, kicking herself for immediately attributing a personal, *sensual* connotation to those words. She was far from desperate sexually, but perhaps she should've gone on a date or two in the past year. Maybe then she wouldn't be so...*aware* of him.

She sucked in a stealthy breath. 'I wouldn't hold your breath, if I were you. I would say, though, that the view from your chalet is exceptional and best enjoyed before the sun goes down. I'll show you the way.'

'Ah, the personal touch. I'm honoured.'

The droll look he sent her told her he knew the game she was playing. That he was willing to play along. For now.

With every cell in her body Amelie wanted to stay behind the reception desk, with the solid, hand-carved polished wenge wood as a sturdy buffer. But that would be as unconscionable as baring her throat to him and inviting him to take a maiming bite.

And why that savage imagery should drag a boatload of heat low in her belly, Amelie refused to ponder, as she briskly rounded the desk and approached him.

'This way.' She indicated the wide arched hallway to their right and watched his gaze fall on the colourful bangles adorning her wrist. Heat flared higher in her belly and she hastened her steps. The quicker this was over, the quicker she could retreat and re-strategize.

She took him down winding paved paths bordered by a profusion of the bold, exotic flowers that were her head gardener's pride and joy. On a normal day she would have literally stopped to smell the roses, but Atu Quayson's solid, unyielding presence behind her overshadowed everything else.

'This is where you make polite chit-chat, isn't it? Or does that courtesy not extend to me?' he drawled.

She stopped in her tracks, then pivoted to face him, all pretence at being unaffected evaporating at his domineering tone and imposing presence. 'Why are you really here?' she snapped, before she could stop herself.

'You turned up uninvited at my office to state your case—'

'So, what? This is payback?'

He shrugged again, his eyes conducting a slow, searing scrutiny of her face that made her want to squirm. To slick her tongue over suddenly tingling lips.

'Perhaps yearning from afar doesn't work for me any longer. I needed to see what I desire up close.'

He was talking about *business*. She knew that. And yet heat funnelled up from her toes, rendering her weak and needy and speechless, making her jaw slacken and her mouth drop open as she stared up at him.

His infuriating male perfection seemed to have multiplied a thousandfold since she'd visited his office.

For a long spell they regarded each other, the

atmosphere snapping with electric currents she feared would zap her if she so much as moved.

'Shall we?' he urged, his gaze sweeping over her lips again before meeting her eyes. 'Unless you wish to invite more gossip by standing here glaring at me?'

Amelie roused herself with self-loathing effort, shuddering to think how much time had passed as she'd stood there, gaping at him.

She whirled and continued down the path, but she couldn't help flinging over her shoulder, 'Don't act like you care about gossip. You knew the commotion you'd create by coming here and you did it anyway.'

'Why, thank you. I wasn't aware I held that sort of power,' he stated drolly.

A sharp pang darted through her chest, his off-hand attitude and arrogance making her voice shake as she snapped, 'Is this all a game to you?'

All traces of humour left his face, replaced by a flinty, narrow-eyed gleam in his eyes that sent different tingles down her spine.

'I don't have time for games, Amelie. I wouldn't need to be here at all if you'd listen to reason. You want me out of your life this badly? Give my proposal the proper consideration it deserves and we won't need to see each other again,' he bit out.

Something about hearing that he'd rather be anywhere else than there stung deeply. Made her twist around and continue down the path leading to his chalet.

She told herself it was no use arguing with him—that his inability to take no for an answer wasn't her problem. If he wanted to pay to stay at her resort, and then leave with the same *no* she'd been saying for months, then on his head be it.

And yet her vision blurred slightly as the chalet came into sight…

The horrifying knowledge that his words had burrowed deep enough to draw tears snapped her spine straight. She hadn't weathered storms of grief, loss and watching her mother sink deeper into the pain of her sister's death to the exclusion of all else just to get emotional over the callous words of a ruthless businessman with only his bottom line in mind.

But he's not just that, is he?

Jaw clenched, she pushed away the fiery reminder as they arrived at the allocated building.

Each chalet had a unique name and symbol carved into its front door. Her breath caught in her throat when Atu reached out and traced his fingers over the *sankofa* symbol that his chalet was named after, depicting a bird retrieving its precious egg. He was admiring the rich wood and intricate workmanship. So why did it feel as if he was stroking her skin?

Probably because that same symbol was also a love symbol...

As if she'd spoken that unacceptable thought out loud, his gaze flicked to her. It held hers for several seconds before, with a smooth swipe of the card, he let the door spring open.

She should leave. She'd done her hospitable duty, after all.

But he waved her in and Amelie found herself entering the room, the charged atmosphere intensifying as he followed close behind.

The panels of the shutters were made of thin strips of woven bamboo, and opened out to let the sea breeze in. The mid-afternoon sun's rays streamed in from the picturesque windows and wide balcony doors. The theme extended to the lamps dotted around the room, and the swinging half-doors that led to the bathroom.

'Ninety per cent of the furnishings in this room are locally sourced,' she said proudly.

His lips twitched. 'As opposed to the mass-market-produced ones you think adorn my hotels?'

'I don't think it. I know it for a fact,' she said,

and then almost kicked herself. Now he knew she'd taken an interest in his hotels.

The twitch turned into the ghost of a smile. 'Local is good and admirable. But I run a global business. Which is why I insist on both local and international sustainability.'

Her eyes widened before she could stop herself.

'You didn't know that?' he mused sardonically. 'And I thought you knew everything about me.'

'I know enough to know what I want. And what I don't.'

His nostrils flared—a sign that he wasn't as amused as he appeared. That some of the capricious atmosphere they'd been unable to escape was finally seeping beneath his guard.

Good. She hoped it sent him packing as quickly as he'd arrived.

The thundering in her chest suggested she might not get her wish as he sauntered over to the cherrywood wardrobe, dropped his weekender into it, then faced her, hands braced on his lean hips.

'This is adequate enough, I suppose,' he said, after a cursory look around.

Knowing he was attempting to rile her only made her fight harder to rise above it. She smiled through a quick tour of the chalet, pointing out the various unique items she'd gone to great lengths over to ensure her guests' comfort.

Done, she faced him once more. 'It's far above "adequate", Mr Quayson. Or are you simply not man enough to admit it?'

The heated gleam in his eyes made her regret her taunt for a mere second before a traitorous sliver of excitement made her wonder how he would react.

His gaze narrowed momentarily, before flicking behind her. Heat ramped through her when she followed his gaze to the sumptuous bed behind her.

'Don't throw down gauntlets that might get you into trouble, Amelie. After all, we don't want to scandalise your precious guests or your beloved townsfolk, do we?'

She cleared her throat, shoved her hands into her pockets so he couldn't see her nails biting into her palms to counter the effect of his words. 'We have a turndown service, if you'd like that. There's a list of every service in the brochure on the dresser—'

'I think I'm content with the finer offerings of your chalet.'

She pinned a professional smile on her face

and headed for the door. 'In that case, I'll leave you to it.'

'Amelie.'

The low rumbled command of her name made her freeze.

'You're sitting on a goldmine here. But from what I've seen, you're nowhere near reaping the full rewards of such a place. I hear you're barely breaking even.'

The dart of pain was unexpected, spiking her agitation all over again. 'You hear wrong,' she countered bravely, hoping he wouldn't spot the lie. 'And you should be careful about using the word *goldmine* around these parts. You don't want to be thrown off the premises before you've had time to sample premium Hayford hospitality.'

Something indecipherable flickered across his features. Then one arrogant eyebrow cocked. 'I can't change the fact that my family owns a goldmine. Or that it's one of the many subjects you and your family find objectionable. It doesn't change the truth. You're hurtling towards the red at breakneck speed, and being stubborn won't get you out of your troubles,' he stated, without an ounce of regret.

She forced herself not to react, despite the constricting of her heart. Despite wanting to rail at fate for all the sorrow and terrifying challenges she'd had to endure because of what he and his family had done to hers.

And, yes, the Fante pride that burned through her blood wouldn't let her back down. He was on her turf. And she didn't intend to give him a single excuse to wrong-foot her.

With that thought in mind, she opened the door, breathed in the sweet ocean air and forced calm into her roiling mind. 'This conversation is over. Now, would you like your complimentary bottle of champagne delivered to you now or later?'

He slipped one hand into his pocket and sauntered towards her, as if he had all the time in the world and had zero qualms about making her wait. 'I'll have it later. With my dinner. Which I'd like you to join me for.'

Amelie tightened her fingers momentarily on the door, then shook her head. 'I'm sorry, but I'll have to decline.'

His lips twitched. 'Do me a favour and drop the niceties. You're not sorry at all. Tell me why,' he ordered, with a bite in his tone.

'I can list a dozen reasons. But the only one pertinent here is that I don't fraternise with guests. Unless you're ready to admit you're not here as a guest but have come to harass me?'

He shrugged broad shoulders that immediately commanded her attention. She allowed herself a mere flicker of a glance before dragging her gaze away. The great thing about her resort was that there was always something spectacular to look at. And in that moment, the sun's rays bouncing off the brilliant red and blue hull of a fisherman's canoe was the perfect tableau to distract herself with.

Definitely *not* the breathtaking tower of a man who was watching her with silent speculation from a few feet away.

Slowly, the humour vanished. 'We both know why I'm here. My advice to you is this—don't make it harder than it needs to be.'

'Here's my answer—your family has done enough damage to mine. So as long as there's breath in my body I'll fight you. And I'll win.'

CHAPTER THREE

THROUGH A COMBINATION of sheer luck and dexterous scheming, Amelie managed to avoid running into Atu at all the next day. But that didn't mean she hadn't caught far too many glimpses of him—starting from the moment she'd woken up.

The one-hundred-and-eighty-degree sea view from her bedroom granted her one of the best views of the sunrise. It was where she enjoyed her morning coffee while running through her day's itinerary.

It was also where she'd choked on her coffee as she'd watched Atu saunter out of the sea at six a.m., his glorious body gleaming under the rising sun's adoring rays like a mythological god.

Even from behind the safety of her whitewashed shutters, the sight of his long, sleek limbs and tempered muscles had made her belly clench and her sex heat in shameless need.

As if he'd sensed her ogling, he'd turned his head towards her window, those probing eyes searching her out, mocking her held breath and the deep awareness charging through her body.

She'd stood her ground and refused to retreat when he'd prowled to the edge of the picket fence boundary between the resort and her home. He hadn't looked up at her window again, seemingly content to enjoy the spectacular sunrise. But she'd suspected he knew she was there.

As aware of her as she was of him.

She'd taken her time to finish her coffee before showering. And if she'd lingered under the cool water in the hopes of dousing the treacherous flames that seemed to take hold of her every time Atu glanced her way, that was her business and no one else's.

She'd been guiltily thankful that her mother wasn't up; that her pain-dulled eyes wouldn't probe hers and somehow discover that Amelie was tolerating their enemy under her resort's roof.

But her secret hopes that her unwanted guest would depart were repeatedly dashed as he made his presence felt continually throughout the day.

She ate her lunch in her office, after seeing him seated in the dining room, casually scrolling through his tablet as he sampled her chef's best dishes.

Mid-afternoon, Maria gleefully informed her that Mr Quayson was enjoying a cocktail at the seafront bar and had signed up for one of the much-loved informal beachfront dinners she threw twice a week for guests.

Amelie had discovered the joy of combining helping the locals offload their day's catch, fresh from the sea, with a seafood-themed dinner, cooked over an open firepit right on the beach, accompanied by music and dancing from a local dance troupe.

As much as she was reluctant to admit it, hosting the dinners had alleviated a little of her loneliness and the stark absence of a relationship—especially as she knew many of her ex-friends from her former prosperous life were in serious relationships, or married with children.

The thought of Atu ruining her organised life made her grind her teeth. And yet, as evening approached, she found herself double-checking her hair and make-up, spritzing on her favourite perfume, while attempting to corral the swarm of butterflies fluttering in her belly before making her way towards the beach.

At the top of the gentle slope leading down to where her staff had set up in preparation for the evening's activities, she stopped and took a deep breath. The air was clean and fresh, the dark caramel-coloured sand inviting her to kick off her shoes and experience its warmth barefoot.

Low, wooden-slatted chairs had been grouped in a wide circle around a large firepit, and on either side of the circle two food stations were manned by professional chefs.

One of the waitstaff spotted her and headed over with a drinks tray. Amelie bypassed the chilled glasses of *nsaafuo*, the locally produced palm wine, in favour of her preferred drink—a mango and guava cocktail laced with ginger and rum. Palm wine had a tendency to go down too easily and sneak up on the unsuspecting with its alcoholic punch.

She needed her wits about her while Atu was around.

Her face burned as she recalled the last time she'd been tipsy around him. She'd not only made a fool of herself, she'd ignored the warning signs that her sister needed her. The ball of sorrow in her stomach made Amelie fear she would live with that regret for the rest of her life.

She mingled with her guests, ignoring the dart of hollow disquiet when she didn't spot Atu. Was she seriously disappointed that he wasn't here? What was wrong with her?

Shaking the feeling off, she threw herself into hostess mode, and soon the mouth-watering smells of grilled seafood and roasting meat were easing the tension that had taken hold of her all day.

Maybe her prayers had been answered and he'd left the resort—

'There you are.'

She started, twisting her head to meet the sardonic dark chocolate gaze of the very man she'd been thinking about. Suddenly the air seemed crisper, the tang of ginger on her tongue sharper. The cool air drifting in from the ocean making her aware of every inch of her skin.

She hated to admit that he made everything so much more vibrant. Made her feel insanely... *alive*.

What did it say about her that her enemy did this to her?

But he hadn't always been her enemy, had he?

Before that fateful weekend she'd harboured a crush that had bloomed into something stronger, more potent. But everything that had come after had shown her those emotions were a mistake, that she should be thankful it hadn't gone beyond a torrid embrace. Like her parents, she'd learned to her cost that the Quaysons, and especially their black sheep, weren't people she wanted to tangle with.

So why couldn't she free herself of those electrifying minutes? Why, even now, did her face trace his chiselled features, lingering far too long on those sensual lips, remembering what it had been like to be devoured by them?

Wishing she could experience it again?

'Cat got your tongue?' he drawled, before his gaze fell to her drink. 'Or is it something else? If I recall, two drinks were your limit.'

And just like that, sparks flew under her skin. She glanced around, thankful that the local troupe's beating of the *kpanlogo* drums was loud enough to drown out his words. 'Not that it's any of your business, but I wasn't drunk that night, and I wouldn't be so distasteful as to fall about drunk in front of my guests now.'

A smile flicked at one corner of his mouth, as if he was enjoying riling her. 'Good to hear.' He sipped his own drink, his gaze conducting a head-to-toe scrutiny. 'Being relaxed looks good on you.'

'Then it's a shame you're here to ruin my vibe.'

His amusement turned into a full-blown smile, making her toes curl deep into the sand and her belly tighten at the transformation of his face.

Dear God, he had no right to look that breathtaking.

When she managed to drag her gaze away, she noticed the avid female looks slanting his way.

Which only made her belly tighten harder, this time in…jealousy?

She shook her head, desperately dissipating that absurd notion.

'I've spent the day interacting with a few of your guests. They speak admirably of your efforts here. You should be proud.'

'I am,' she replied, unable to stem the warmth flooding her at his words. But then she caught herself and forced a glare his way. 'If you feel that way, why are you trying to take it away?'

Frustration and that ever-present hint of ruthlessness flickered over his chiselled face. 'Because I've also seen that beneath the shine and gloss things are beginning to fray at the edges. You need an injection of serious capital, and fast. Are you going to deny it?'

She pressed her lips together, refusing to answer.

Impatience flitted over his face. 'This place can be world-class, Amelie. With every advantage and success at your fingertips. The Quayson Group can make that happen.'

'Sure, while stamping your name all over it.'

The hardness in his eyes intensified, and that foolish shred of hope attempting to flare to life died a quick death.

'It's the only way. A partnership between us would never work,' he said.

Why did that sting so much? For a single moment she hated the feud which had dogged their families. Then she reminded herself who was behind it and hardened her emotions.

'I see the shutters coming down,' he bit out derisively.

'No, what you see is me reminding you again that this conversation is inappropriate—now or at any time in the future.'

That earned her a narrow-eyed look of mockery. 'I'm beginning to think you enjoy butting heads with me.'

The intuitive remark about something she'd been denying since their heated exchange in his office startled her. But before she could summon an adequately cutting response, she heard her name being called out.

Even before she turned, she was dreading confirmation of the owner of that voice.

Sure enough, Joyce Blankson, a wealthy socialite and one-time close friend of her parents, was making her way gingerly through the sand.

Amelie groaned under her breath.

'Something wrong?' Atu asked.

She shook her head, refusing to lose even more

of her composure. 'I think my vibe is about to be ruined even further.'

'Amelie, there you are. I was hoping I'd run into you this weekend,' Joyce said, brazen curiosity in the gaze darting between her and Atu.

'Good evening, Auntie.' Although the woman was no blood relation, Amelie used the respectful term afforded older folk. 'I hope my staff are looking after you?'

The woman, who had delicate, birdlike features, gestured with bejewelled fingers. 'Of course they are. Your exemplary service is the reason I keep returning.'

That and gathering as much gossip as she could to relate to her friends in the city. The wealthy socialite thrived on ferreting out people's deepest, darkest secrets and sharing them with whoever would listen.

Amelie's mother had once stated that Joyce would befriend a shiver of sharks if it got her the latest gossip.

'Thank you, Auntie,' she replied politely.

Joyce eyed Atu in open speculation. 'You're the last person I expected to see here.'

She sensed Atu stiffen, but his faintly forbidding expression didn't alter. 'Am I?' he answered coolly.

Joyce waved her hand again, making the expensive bangles on her wrist tinkle. 'Every person in this country knows your two families don't mix. Which makes me wonder why you're at this resort at all—never mind socialising with a Hayford.'

For a moment Amelie wished she'd stayed in her office, instead of coming out here to show Atu that she wouldn't be intimidated into avoiding him in her own resort.

It was too late now. The proverbial cat was out of the bag.

Atu sent Joyce a thin, humourless smile which made the older woman blink warily. 'I believe that's my business, Auntie. Can we help you with anything else?' he asked, not bothering to thaw the layer of ice in his tone.

Joyce's lips pursed. Sending him an approving glance, she spun on her heel and walked away.

'Do you know what you've done?' Amelie sniped, while attempting to keep her smile in place.

'Refused to lower myself to idle gossip?'

'You've ensured that news of your presence here will be all over the country by morning.'

His eyes narrowed. 'I thought I'd already done that by turning up in the first place?'

As if drawn by a magnet, her gaze swung towards her home, her teeth worrying her lower lip.

'Your mother still doesn't know I'm here, does she?' he intuited accurately.

Amelie sucked in a breath. 'I haven't seen the need to inform her of your visit, no.'

'So you'd rather she heard it from Accra's biggest gossip?' he demanded, eyeing the older woman, who even now was sending them surreptitious glances from a distance.

It was a miracle her mother hadn't already discovered the ever-increasing pressure being put on her by the Quayson Group.

Pain rippled through her as she acknowledged why. While her father had been alive her mother had had something to live for, despite the demise of her much-beloved eldest daughter. With him gone, her once-vibrant mother had withdrawn deeper into herself, and the presence of her youngest remaining child had done nothing to pierce her veil of grief.

'I'll tell her in my own time,' she responded, her vehemence from before curiously absent. If her mother found out about Atu's visit, and his family's unrelenting efforts to acquire their resort, it would break her—perhaps irreparably.

She looked up, and found him watching her

with a pensiveness that made the breath snag in her throat. She was struck with a wild urge to plead with him to leave her and her family alone.

An intense look entered his eyes just then, as if he'd read her thoughts. As if he *wanted* to hear her beg.

Aware of eyes watching them—especially Joyce's—she took a step back from him. 'I need to attend to my guests. Enjoy the rest of your evening, Mr Quayson.'

His jaw gritted for a moment. Then his fierce expression eased.

She didn't fool herself into thinking she'd escaped scot-free.

For the rest of the evening she ensured she remained outside his immediate orbit, and despite sending her a few levelling glances, he didn't venture any closer.

But even as she left her guests with endorsements of another successful evening ringing in her ears, she knew she was only prolonging the inevitable—both with her mother and with Atu.

When she found herself still awake after midnight, tossing and turning, she was frustrated but not surprised. She was also a little ashamed at the relief she'd felt when the housekeeper reported that her mother hadn't left her room all day, or taken any calls.

Before retiring to bed, Amelie had stood outside her mother's room, gnawing on her lip as she contemplated telling her about Atu. The thought of bringing further pain had made her shy away, even as she'd berated herself for ignoring a looming problem.

Wouldn't her mother be proud of her if she succeeded in sending Atu packing?

And then what?

Those three words eventually dragged her out of bed and onto the quiet stretch of beach.

The moon hung low, creating a wide beam of light over the still ocean. Just like the beauty of sunset, experiencing the serenity under moonlight reminded her of how much she loved her little corner of the earth. How hard she was willing to fight to hang on to it.

But how?

Half-formed solutions darted through her brain, each one less feasible than the last.

Lost in thought, she didn't notice she'd approached the border between her home and the resort until she looked up.

Into the eyes of Atu Quayson.

She had a fleeting urge to turn around, to rush

back to the safety of her bedroom. But her feet refused to obey that thought. Then her stubbornness kicked in.

'What are you doing here?' she asked.

He shoved his hands into the pockets of his linen trousers, stretching the material across his taut thighs.

Not that she was looking.

'I couldn't sleep. From the looks of it, neither could you.'

He approached as he spoke, and this close, his presence overwhelmed her. Reminded her of the thinness of the sleeveless thigh-skimming tunic she'd thrown on to come out. And the fact that she was only wearing a flimsy thong underneath.

She folded her arms across her chest as a cool breeze blew over her.

Ruthless impatience flitted over his face. 'There's one simple way to end this.'

Days of frustration threatened to boil over. 'Have you stopped for a moment to think what this might do to my mother?'

His jaw tightened for a moment and she thought she spotted a hint of regret in his eyes before she admitted she was deluding herself. Because when his gaze fixed on her, it was the harsh regard of an apex predator unwilling to consider the frivolous emotions of its prey.

'I don't deal in sentiment, Amelie. This is business—pure and simple.'

'Silly me. Of course you don't. And I don't remember inviting you to use my name.'

'Don't you?' he enquired silkily. 'Maybe not recently, but I recall you wishing I would on another occasion.'

Her next breath evaporated from her lungs. 'Your memory might be faulty.'

A sardonic gleam lit through his eyes. 'Don't shame us both by pretending you don't know what I'm talking about.'

Her heart hammered against her ribs. Did he remember their encounter as intensely as she did?

'Yes, I remember,' he said, as if she'd asked the question aloud.

She wrapped her arms around her middle and raised her chin. 'Whatever you think you remember, we both know it meant nothing. Let's leave it buried in the past where it belongs.'

For a moment he looked furious. Offended. He took a single step towards her, determination in his stance.

'But is it, though?' Before she could answer,

he continued. 'Because it feels like it's right here between us. Getting in our way.'

'This may just mean business to you, but don't you get it? It's all *personal* to me. Every grain of sand on this beach, every leaf on every palm tree means something to me. But then that's your way, isn't it? First your brother—now you've come to finish the job.'

His eyes narrowed into dangerous slits. 'What exactly do you believe my brother did?' His voice was a sheet of thin ice over a frozen lake. Ominous and dangerous.

She refused to back down. 'What you're doing now! You see something you want and you do everything in your power to take it, regardless of the distress you cause.'

'Attaching sentiment to professional dealings is a bad business model.'

'While your problem is attaching none! Even if I wanted to, why would I allow an emotionless automaton to take charge of what I hold most dear?'

'Did you believe I was so unfeeling when you threw yourself at me eight years ago? When you were busy getting what you wanted from me?'

'Excuse me?'

'No, you're not excused,' he condemned harshly.

'You were good at blinding me—I must give you that. But if you're throwing blame around, have the decency to take your fair share. You saw something you wanted—me—and you went for it, didn't you?'

She gasped. 'How dare you?'

'Amelie—'

'No!' She batted away his warning, years of pain, grief and anger congealing into a tight ball inside her. 'Haven't you taken enough? Why this resort? Why not one of the thousands anywhere else in the world?'

She hated that her voice emerged shakily. That even now she couldn't dismiss him as callously as she wanted to. That a part of her still wished all the acrimony between them didn't exist.

So that what? So she could throw herself in his arms the way she couldn't seem to stop imagining doing every time he was within touching distance?

'Because I'm the devil you know,' he rasped chillingly.

She froze in place. 'What's that supposed to mean?'

He shook his head. 'Tell me what you meant about Fiifi,' he gritted out, completely ignoring her question and her other indictments.

For a moment she regretted bringing up his dead brother. For dredging up memories they'd both rather forget. 'I hate to speak ill of the dead, but do you deny that had he been alive he wouldn't be doing the same thing you're doing now?'

An emotion closely resembling anguish lanced across his face, then was swiftly extinguished. 'You seemed determined to tar every member of my family with the same villain's brush. Have you considered that, were he alive, all this animosity might have been resolved by now?'

In her lowest times she fooled herself into considering that. Then she was reminded that their families had been well set on enmity long before they'd lost their respective siblings. And, hell, the Quaysons had even revelled in their superiority.

'I don't believe that. Not when—'

'When what?' he snapped.

The knot in her stomach grew. 'The apple doesn't fall far from the tree, so of course Fiifi was acting the typical Quayson, but you were there that night. You knew something was seriously wrong. And he'd upset my sister before the party...'

He stiffened. 'What are you trying to say, Amelie?'

'That maybe you…we…could've done something. Instead of…'

'Instead of allowing ourselves to be distracted? Or is the blame one-sided?'

She shrugged. 'If you hadn't dragged me away—'

His harsh laugh froze her accusation. 'You can rewrite history all you want, sweet Amelie, but you came willingly. You were as eager to taste me as I was to satisfy that wide-eyed hunger you did such a poor job of hiding.'

His eyes narrowed, but she caught the flash of smugness within.

'Tell me, was I your first kiss?'

She turned, blindly stalking towards the gate.

Firm hands cupped her shoulders, stalling her flight. 'The truth is difficult to swallow, isn't it?'

'Stop it!'

The words were as much for her as for him. Because while she'd kissed a few boys previously, the kiss they'd shared had shown her a far superior realm of passion she'd never forgotten or duplicated. And, yes, she hated him a little for that.

'Let me go,' she rasped, doing her utmost to ignore the heat of his touch branding her, making her feel things she didn't want to but couldn't stop yearning for.

'Why? So you can run away? So you can slide between your sheets, smug with your righteous indignation?'

She tore herself free of his hold and whirled to confront him. 'No, so I can pretend you don't exist for a few blessed hours.'

For a moment a bleak look scraped across his face. Then he gathered himself with a formidable willpower she secretly envied.

'As regrettable as that incident was, burying our heads in the sand this time won't make any of this go away.'

A cold shiver washed over her, and it had nothing to do with the breeze coming off the ocean. 'You regret it?' she blurted, before she could stop herself.

One eyebrow rose mockingly. 'Don't you? Isn't that what all this extra animosity aimed at me in particular is all about?'

He was giving her the perfect out. She drew in a shaky breath and took it, ignoring the hollow in her gut. Ignoring the vice tightening curiously around her chest.

'You're right. It was a mistake.'

He stared at her for a charged moment, then

turned his profile towards the ocean, leaving her to collect her tattered composure.

Another breeze washed over her and she shivered.

His gaze swung to her and she knew he hadn't missed her reaction. Within one moment and the next he was shrugging off his shirt.

'Wh-what are you doing?' she blurted as he came towards her.

Another mirthless twist of his lips. 'You may believe I'm your enemy, but I don't want you catching cold and falling ill. Or worse.'

She aimed a glare his way. 'Not until I've signed on whatever dotted line you're determined to foist upon me, you mean?'

That look of fury returned. This time accompanied by a flash of disappointment. As if he had a right to such a lofty emotion where she was concerned.

She tried to summon her own outrage, grinding her teeth when she failed miserably because all she could feel was the warmth from his shirt as he draped it over her shoulders. All she could smell when she took a breath was the scent of his aftershave and that unique brand of masculinity that had drawn her like the proverbial moth to a flame ever since she hit puberty and crossed that forbidden line from family friend to something...*more*.

She wanted—no, *needed* to refuse this small offer of comfort.

Hand him back his shirt. Leave the beach.

Return to her room and come up with a definite plan that removed him from her life for good.

So why was she drawing the flaps of his shirt closer? Why were her fingers clinging to the warm cotton as if she'd never let it go?

Why were her eyes drawn to the torso moulded by the pristine white T-shirt he wore underneath the shirt?

Her gaze lingered on the outline of the chiselled six-pack, dropping lower to the faint bulge at the front of his linen trousers, her breath catching all over again at the memory of his arousal against her belly that weekend, when they'd given in to temptation, oh, so briefly...

She must have made a sound at the back of her throat, because his head swung towards her, his eyes holding hers for an age before he exhaled harshly.

His lips firmed and for a long stretch he didn't speak. Then, 'You need to accept that I'm the best bet you have right now. I'm going to win eventually. How soon depends entirely on you.'

His implacable conclusion sent icy shivers coursing through her. In that moment, she regretted every moment of weakness. Regretted feeling bad for evoking that hint of disappointment in his eyes.

She had nothing to be ashamed of. Not when vanquishing her and her family was his true purpose.

She snatched his shirt from her shoulders, crushing her body's instant insistence on its warmth as she tossed it back to him. 'You should know by now that threats don't faze me. We're still here, still standing, after all you and your family have done. So go ahead—do your worst.'

Head held high, she whirled away.

She only made it three steps before he captured her wrist. She spun around, intent on pushing him away. But that ruthlessness was coupled with something else. Something hot and blazing and all-consuming in his eyes.

She belatedly read it as lust just before he tugged her closer, wrapping one hand around her waist and the other in her hair.

'This stubborn determination is admirable. Hell, I'd go so far as to say it's a turn-on, because God knows I admire strong, wilful women,' he muttered, his lips a hair's breadth from hers. 'But fiery passion will only get you so far.'

'And what are you going to do about it?' she taunted, a little too breathlessly. Every cell in her body traitorously strained towards him, yearning for things she knew she shouldn't want, but desperately needed anyway.

He froze, and then, with a strangled sound leaving his throat, he slammed his lips on hers.

Just like those charged pockets of time that had trapped them sporadically since his arrival, time seemed suspended in static electricity as his lips devoured hers.

There was nothing apologetic or hesitant about Atu's kiss.

He kissed her as if he was starved for it. *For her.*

And, heaven help her, after fighting and craving this insane chemistry in equal measure for days…*years*…the battle went out of her.

She surrendered with a broken moan which he immediately pounced on, parting her lips with his and brazenly stroking her tongue with his.

Static electricity turned to dangerous, thrilling lightning, sending decadent shivers coursing through her body. Her senses blazed as he pulled her deeper into his arms, wrapping his heat around her while he tasted her over and over.

And then, as swiftly as it had arrived, the spell was broken by the crest of a wave washing over their feet.

She gasped, then shuddered as reality harshly intruded.

Even then she was reluctant to pull away from his warmth, from the hypnotic kiss. A kiss that was a world away from the one they'd shared all those years ago. But it turned out *that* kiss had been a precursor...a delightful appetiser before a decadent main course which she'd merely sampled.

And as she stared up into his face, at the far too chiselled perfection of her enemy, she wanted to throw caution and every last sane thought away and experience it again.

The potency of that need made her wrench herself free from him, her body shaking as she stumbled a few necessary steps back.

Self-preservation insisted she salvage the moment. She opened her mouth. 'You... You...' Then she cringed as words failed her.

Eyes hot and alive with lust only moments ago cooled, the faintest grimace darting over his face before his features settled into a haughty mask. 'I'm sorry. That shouldn't have happened.'

Dear God. He regretted this kiss too...

The hazy, heady emotion receded, leaving her nonplussed. But then a shot of feminine power restored her equilibrium. Because while he might be regretting it, his body supplied ample evidence of what their kiss had done to him—mostly below his belt and in the unevenness of his breathing.

Still, she wasn't about to show her bewilderment. 'You're right. It was a mistake,' she said, even as she inhaled his scent from the shirt that had somehow found its way back onto her shoulders, keeping her warm in the cool air.

That increasingly riveting twist of his lips appeared again. 'I said it shouldn't have happened. I didn't say it was a mistake.'

A dull throb at her temples told her she needed to retreat. Attempt to regroup. But then how many times had she done that in recent days? And how well had it worked?

'Meet with me tomorrow, Amelie.'

She opened her mouth, automatic refusal surging. But over his shoulder a light flicked on in the top left corner of her house. Her mother's bedroom light.

She swallowed, the thought of being discovered on the beach with Atu sending trepidation dancing in her belly.

He followed her gaze. Then his eyes narrowed

on her face. 'One hour. Let's discuss this properly once and for all.'

Amelie knew better than to insist he leave her resort after that hour. She suspected he was about to unleash the big guns. Wasn't she better off meeting him and arming herself instead of being taken by surprise by his next move?

His gaze remained locked on hers, his body solid and immovable in front of her, as if he had all the time in the world. And in this instance, didn't he? Wasn't she the one facing another fiscal quarter of intense challenges unless she came up with a miracle?

'Fine. Eight o'clock tomorrow morning. My office,' she offered briskly.

He shook his head. 'I have other business in the morning, and I'd prefer somewhere we're not interrupted. I've booked your private chef service for tomorrow. I'll have him prepare us a meal in my chalet.'

His faintly raised eyebrow dared her to object. The thought of being alone with him sent frissons of foolish excitement coursing through her body. But she'd wasted enough time on this beach, beating her head against the brick wall of his resistance. Not to mention that completely inappropriate, earth-shaking kiss…

'Amelie.'

Steel edged his voice. As if, like her, he was reaching the end of his endurance.

Another light came on—this time in the living room downstairs. Her mother was looking for her.

'Fine. Dinner. I'll be there.'

She ignored the flare of triumph in his eyes.

'Sleep well, Amelie.'

She didn't respond because she knew she wouldn't.

Instead, she attempted to shove her roiling emotions away as she re-entered her home.

Her mother was wearing a long nightgown with a robe thrown over it. Amelie's heart lurched as she took in her stooped, grief-shrouded form as she stood staring at her sister's portrait.

'Maa?'

She turned, her eyes momentarily blank before settling on her. 'Where were you?'

'I went for a walk on the beach.'

A frown creased her mother's forehead. 'At this time of night?'

Amelie started to shrug, then froze when the faint aftershave of the man she'd been kissing filled her nostrils.

Her heart banging against her ribs, she bit the inside of her lip when her mother's gaze shifted to the shirt, her frown intensifying.

Her mother opened her mouth, most likely to demand why she was wearing a man's shirt, but Amelie spoke hastily. 'We need to talk, Maa.'

'About what?'

'About the resort.'

Weariness and grief settled more heavily on her mother's shoulders. 'You're in charge of it now, Amelie. Whatever it is…handle it.'

As much as she wanted to grasp that lifeline, she knew her mother wouldn't forgive her once she discovered her involvement—albeit reluctant—with the enemy.

'You need to know what's going on.'

Her mother half-heartedly waved a hand at her, her gaze drifting back to the portrait on the wall. 'It can wait till tomorrow,' she said, with surprisingly firm dismissal.

Amelie stared at her for a moment longer, wishing her heart didn't ache with the pain of being completely ignored by a mother who grieved for her child as if she was the parent to one and not two children. As if she, Amelie, had died too the night her older sister had perished in that car crash.

CHAPTER FOUR

'WE HAVE A PROBLEM.'

Amelie stopped herself from groaning as Maria entered her office. Every instinct said that whatever the problem was involved Atu Quayson. She knew he was a problem for her. She hadn't been able to stop thinking about him all day. He'd invaded her thoughts during her meetings, with those sizzling minutes in his arms, his mouth on hers, replaying in her brain on an endless loop.

Oh, yes, she laid the blame for her complete lack of concentration firmly at his feet.

'We do?' she answered, forcing the memories from her mind. And failing.

Maria's face contorted in a grimace. 'We're short-staffed in the spa. Dzifa has a family emergency. I've had to send her home.'

Amelie nodded, almost welcoming the chance to *not* think about Atu Quayson for a fraction of a second. Not to think of their charged conversation on the beach and the kiss afterwards.

She also didn't want to recall that her mother had left instructions with the housekeeper this morning that she wasn't to be disturbed, even by her daughter, thus ensuring their talk wouldn't happen today.

What did it say about her that she'd rather face a staff shortage problem than deal with the hard knot of pain and desolation that came with her mother's rejection?

'Okay. So let's move some other staff around. We have two more masseurs, don't we?'

Maria shook her head. 'They're fully booked for the next four hours. And we have a VIP appointment that can't be moved.'

Something in her manager's tone captured her attention. 'Who's the VIP?'

Maria stared steadily at her. 'Who do you think?'

For the smallest, most shameful instant, Amelie was pleased her head masseur was unavailable. Because the thought of someone else's hands on Atu's body triggered an emotion that absurdly resembled jealousy.

You're losing it...

'Mr Quayson's appointment is in...' Maria glanced at her watch and sighed. 'Nineteen minutes.'

Amelie massaged the bridge of her nose, the sensation of being caught in the fabled spiderweb of Ananse the Trickster of native Akan folklore closing over her.

'Amelie? You don't want me to cancel, do you?' Maria pressed with quiet urgency.

She firmed her lips to stop the *yes* she yearned to say from spilling free. 'No, I don't.'

Maria gave a brisk nod, but continued to stare at her.

After several seconds, Amelie raised her eyebrow. 'Was there something else?'

'No, that's it. But, just to be clear, *you're* taking the appointment, right?' Maria asked. 'Or will you swap with one of the other girls?'

Heat swept through her—which she quickly banished before it took hold. A situation like this was why she'd taken a massage course three years ago. This wouldn't be the first time she'd stepped into a different role besides the one marked *Resort Director* on her office door.

Putting her degree in hospitality to good use had taught her to be versatile to daily demands, especially the challenges of juggling tight finances.

'I'll take the appointment.'

Even if that means touching him? Again?

'You sure?'

'I'll be there in ten minutes,' she said firmly.

After a probing look, Maria left, leaving Ame-

lie with a belly quivering with trepidation and…
anticipation.

No, not anticipation.

What had happened on the beach last night couldn't happen again.

So why, after retreating to her bed last night, only to spend hours tossing and turning and re-playing their conversation about the family feud, those charged accusations, and that kiss, had she grabbed her laptop to try and discover more about Atu Quayson?

Because his reaction to her words had been… unexpected. His disappointment. That bleakness. And, yes, even that flash of anguish had thrown her. Enough for her to contemplate—for the brief-est minute—the possibility of accepting his offer.

But how could she?

As much as he mocked her emotional attach-ment to her business decisions, she couldn't sepa-rate herself from it. Considering his offer would decimate her mother. Besides, at no point last night had he denied feeling the same unease about the night of that party.

She'd known her sister was upset, that her and Fiifi's gaiety had felt…*forced.* It had been hiding an underlying unhappiness which they'd covered up with excessive drinking before the fiery crash that had killed them.

Had Atu known that when he'd led her away from the party and into that sizzling embrace that had wiped her mind of everything else?

While she knew she couldn't absolve herself from culpability, had he used her to cover his own demons that night?

The breath shuddered out of her as the possibility settled into her bones, reaffirming the impossibility of considering his proposal. Because in doing so, wouldn't she be betraying her sister once again?

Ignoring the cold bleakness trawling through her, she yanked open a drawer, took out his laundered shirt.

She made her way to the spa, ignoring the inquisitive looks from guests and staff. *Just a few days longer*, she repeated under her breath, as she set out the sensual aromatic oils. Atu Quayson couldn't stay here for ever.

But he *could* fill a room with his presence, she accepted resentfully, when he walked into the spa minutes later. All female eyes tracked him with an avidity that rekindled her irritation.

His dark green short-sleeved shirt showed off brawny arms, the buttons undone drawing attention to his strong throat and smooth chest. His linen trousers gave the impression he was fully embracing the casual resort life, but she wasn't fooled.

He took his time to survey the room, his incisive gaze missing nothing. Seeing his lack of surprise at her presence, Amelie wondered if he'd known about her absent staff. He seemed to know everything else that happened around here, after all.

When he made a beeline for her, his gaze fixing on hers with laser-like intensity, she was almost convinced of it.

'I'm your three o'clock, I believe?' he drawled, his eyes lowering to rest on her mouth for two heartbeats.

She fought to maintain her composure. 'Yes, you are. If you'd like to come with me?'

She dragged her gaze from his heated one that said he was reliving their kiss. That her attempt at stiff formality merely amused him.

'Did you sleep well?' he asked as they entered the VIP spa room furthest from Reception.

She cast what she hoped was a carefree glance over her shoulder. 'Like a baby, thanks.'

His derisory look challenged her answer.

She brazened it out and headed for the preparation table. 'Make yourself comfortable. I won't be a minute.'

Setting out the oils and choosing soothing music to accompany the session put her nerves on edge. Lowering the lights to create the right ambience suddenly made it all feel much too intimate.

Get yourself together!

Finishing quickly, she turned, fixing her gaze just past his left shoulder. 'I'll just step out and let you get ready.'

'No need. I haven't had the misfortune of being labelled a prude yet. Besides, you've seen me in less before. Or was that not you, watching me from your bedroom window yesterday?'

She chose silence, and tried to ignore her tingling senses when he started undoing his shirt.

'Not to stereotype, but I wouldn't have taken you for the massage-loving type,' she blurted, mostly in a wild bid to dissipate the thickening atmosphere.

He shrugged. 'I've learned that a well-skilled massage isn't without its benefits. Besides, my mother tells me I should relax more.'

She opened her mouth to ask after his mother, and then pressed her lips shut. That near-slip made her heart thud in her chest. Sweet heaven, her mother would call her a traitor. Or worse.

'You *can* ask after her, you know. It's not a cardinal sin.'

She flicked her gaze to him, expecting another sardonic look. Instead, he regarded her steadily, with an almost encouraging look in his eyes.

She shook her head. 'What's the point?'

His eyes hardened a touch. 'The point is you were her favourite godchild.'

Her heart lurched in remembrance of the affection his mother had showered on her as a child. Before everything had turned to sorrow and ash.

'It didn't feel like it when our parents were declaring war on each other after…after the accident. And following through on it, I might add.'

Joseph Quayson had ruthlessly wielded his power within days of the double funeral, decimating what had remained of the Hayford businesses until her father had had no choice but to sell all his smaller interests and relocate his family to Saltpond.

Again, she expected a cutting response, but all Atu did was nod. 'Heavy and unexpected loss has a way of bringing out the worst in all of us,' he said cryptically.

She frowned, trying to read his expression, but it remained veiled, and his usually sensual lips were set in a thin line. She yearned to ask him what he'd meant last night about going with the devil she knew. Whether all those years ago he'd deliberately aided the distraction that had taken their attention from their siblings.

But all of a sudden she feared his answer. Feared that she couldn't endure another layer of the guilt she already felt. So she remained silent.

'As much as it makes you feel better to put a barrier between us, we will always have a connection, Amelie,' he said into a silence broken only by the tinkling Tahitian music playing in the background. 'And I, for one, won't pretend it doesn't exist.'

The rasped warning made her go cold, then hot, her heart striking a runaway rhythm again. Because she'd experienced that visceral connection last night. Had been unable to think of little else since…

'Are you ready? I'd like to get on with it, if you don't mind?'

Without answering, he shrugged off his shirt.

Her mouth went dry as heat flooded her.

Yes, she'd seen him stride godlike out of the ocean yesterday, wearing only brief swim-shorts. But that had been from a safe distance.

And, yes, she'd also spent time lazing around

the pool at his lavish family home when her sister and his brother had been alive.

But that had been a time of foolish crushes and girlish dreams.

A time before tragedy struck.

This... *This* was something else.

And then he casually stepped out of his trousers, leaving him clad only in black cotton boxers, and she forgot how to breathe properly.

Not even her wild girlish dreams had done an adequate job of preparing her for the up-close perfection of Atu's body. There wasn't a spare ounce of flesh anywhere on his sleek, well-muscled frame. His six-pack made her fingers burn to touch him. His thighs and calves were thick without looking as if they were out of a bodybuilder's catalogue. Hell, even his feet were a work of art, and she wasn't a huge fan of feet.

When he walked past her towards the massage table, she couldn't help but ogle his tight buttocks. She didn't realise she was locked in place next to the prep station until he glanced over at her, one eyebrow quirked in mild amusement.

The bastard knew exactly what he did to her.

'Amelie.'

'Y-yes?' She cringed at her husky stuttering.

'Relax.'

She blew out a half-irritated, half-control-seeking breath, hating him for his conceited confidence in his perfection.

Before she could direct him, he lay face-down on the table.

Somehow she summoned enough professionalism to do the job.

To her eternal gratitude, he didn't indulge in chit-chat as she worked on his back, thighs and calves. But when he flipped over, Amelie couldn't hide from his steady, unabashed scrutiny. She ignored her hammering heart, the blood rushing too fast through her veins, and hastily moved away when she was done, telling herself that she didn't miss the feel of his smooth muscles beneath her fingertips, the warmth of his flesh or the satisfaction of easing his tense muscles.

She hadn't compromised her professionalism by jumping his bones.

She clung to that as she turned around—only to lose the smile she'd pinned on her face. He'd pulled on his trousers but his shirt remained draped over the chair. And he was watching her with that insane intensity.

'Stop looking at me like that.' Her attempted snap came out more like a breathless plea.

'Like what? Like you're the woman I kissed last

night who kissed me back? The woman who's dying to deny the chemistry between us at all costs? Are you going to continue to bury your head in the sand?'

His words stung. 'It's called being a professional.'

She was surprised when he nodded in agreement. 'And I commend you for it. But our history goes beyond professionalism. This thing's been following us for eight years. Perhaps we need to put it to bed once and for all?'

A charged sound escaped her before she could stop it. And when she opened her mouth he beat her to it.

'If you're about to deny it, save your breath.'

She balled her hands until her fingers bit into her palms. 'I was about to say it doesn't matter. One of us needs to keep a level head.'

His mouth twitched, but humour was missing from his eyes. 'I've never kept a level head around you, Amelie.'

She gasped, her gaze locking on his of its own volition. His eyes smouldered with heat she knew would singe if she ventured closer. And yet she couldn't resist testing its warmth.

He reached out and snagged her wrist, firmly but gently tugging her close until she was trapped between those thighs she'd ogled only a short time ago. She could break his hold and march out the door...but, again, she didn't want to.

One small step, then another, pressed her up against him. The scent of the massage oils combined with his unique scent pulsed all around them, creating a sensual, aromatic cocoon she didn't want to rupture.

A shamefully needy and helpless sound broke from her throat when his gaze dropped to her mouth, his hunger a blatant statement.

'Kiss me,' he commanded, in a low, hypnotic voice.

'Atu...'

Again, his lips twisted... Again, they were absent of humour. 'You whispered my name just like that that night. Do you remember?'

Automatic denial rose to her throat, but it felt like sacrilege to deny that moment. It had changed everything for every one of them. Two families had been shattered, the destinies of two dynasties altered for ever.

His gaze flicked between her mouth and her eyes, burning with a fever she wanted to consume her.

'Don't deny it,' he commanded again.

'Is this your idea of putting this thing to bed?'

Shadows of the haunted look she'd seen that night eight years ago lurked. 'No. I should've specified that pun was very much intended,' he delivered thickly.

'Why...?' Amelie wasn't sure what she was asking.

For several moments he didn't reply. Then, 'Because there are some ghosts we can never lay to rest. But this needn't be one of them.'

'What are you saying? That a kiss will work this out of our systems?'

She couldn't disguise the need in her voice.

He heard it.

Far too arrogant satisfaction eased over his face as he nudged her closer. 'It's a start. Let's find out, shall we?'

With undeniable compulsion, she draped her free hand over his shoulder, then gasped when he brushed his lips over the sensitive skin in the crook of her elbow.

Untamed wildfire blazed through her veins. When she shuddered, he repeated the action, then settled back to watch her, his smugness intensifying when she remained still, silently yearning for more.

Slowly, his other hand curved around her waist,

holding her in place, then caressed lower to grip her hip.

'I'm waiting, Amelie,' he drawled, and the vein of authority in his voice made her shiver. 'You're not evoking fire and brimstone on my head… your breathing is short, sweet and sexy…and you haven't stopped licking your lower lip in anticipation since I asked to taste you. So I'm guessing you want this too,' he stated.

It was the kind of confidence that usually irritated her. Instead, her core clenched with desire, the peaks of her tingling breasts tightening painfully against her dress.

Since he'd swaggered back into her life, she'd striven to resist him at all costs. But Atu Quayson was an unstoppable force of nature. He made her want to scream in frustration and moan with a need she hadn't felt in a very long time. And, yes, even while she despised herself, in the knowledge that perhaps when her sister had needed her most she'd been spellbound by him, she couldn't deny this insanity she'd only ever experienced with him.

He was also the last person she should be craving—for a million reasons. Yet none of those reasons mattered now. Not when he was so close, so…*vital*. Not when every cell in her body yearned for one small taste.

And what if he was right? What if she could rid herself of this desperation once and for all?

'For the love of God, do it before one of us expires from the suspense,' he growled, his lips a hair's breadth from hers.

With a strangled moan ripped from her soul, she surged up and sealed her mouth to his.

He gave a gruff sound of satisfaction, his hand tightening on her hip while the other captured her nape. He allowed her to explore him, savouring the smooth yet firm texture of his full lips, the power in the arms that held her, for all of a minute. Then he took control, parting his lips to invade hers with his tongue.

Atu explored her with unabashed hunger, devouring her as he pulled her closer, until they were half splayed over the massage table. He gave another groan of approval as her breasts connected with his naked torso. Not even the fleeting thought that she'd leave this room with oil stains all over her dress was enough to pull her away from the sensational magic of his thrilling kiss. Her moans mixed with the tinkling of soothing music and his occasional groan as they found new ways of pleasuring each other, of stoking a hunger that always hovered far too close for comfort.

But then she'd never associated comfort with this man.

He was dangerous to her in every way. Private. Professional. *Emotional.*

That final reminder made her jerk away from him, taking several self-preserving steps back. She shut her eyes, her chest heaving as dismay filled her, opening them when she heard him move.

Sweet heaven. What was wrong with her?

His eyes narrowed as he breached the gap between them. 'If you're thinking about coming up with some spurious excuse to cancel dinner with me tonight because of what just happened, forget it,' he warned her tightly.

She pushed against his chest. He resisted for a fraction of a second before he stepped back, but his eyes remained on her. Demanding. Domineering.

'If that's what it takes to get you out of my hair, I'll keep our dinner appointment.'

Satisfaction flashed through his eyes before he walked over to snag his shirt, slipping it back on with an animalistic grace that had her biting back another moan.

She needed to get out of here before she compounded her questionable behaviour by jumping
him again. Since the usual professional courte-
sies seemed inane, in light of what they'd done,
she headed for the door without a word.

'Amelie?'

She pivoted to face him, her racing heart speeding up even further.

'You give a good massage.'

Her face burned. 'I hope if you leave a review
you won't make any comments about what happened *after* your massage.'

Any semblance of civility left his face as it
tightened. 'One of these days your need to cast
me as the villain might get you into more trouble
than you can handle.'

Why the hell did that threat only light up a fire
in her pelvis? Maybe because somewhere deep in
her psyche she knew the kind of trouble he meant
would never be unwelcome? Even now, as displeasure tautened his face, the live wire of their
chemistry continued to sizzle and twist its way
between them, demanding attention.

'You created your own notoriety by labelling
yourself the black sheep of the family. Don't
blame me for believing the evidence you present,' she replied.

But as she walked away she couldn't ignore the flash of shame she experienced. Because he was right. She was clinging to every bad impression she'd formed about him to put a barrier between them, while her own decisions kept weakening it.

But wasn't the alternative an even scarier prospect?

Because didn't she suspect that the crush she'd always harboured for Atu Quayson might have morphed into something more dangerous, more life-altering?

Just...*more*?

Seven o'clock arrived far too quickly. And as she approached Atu's chalet, she asked herself for the millionth time if she was doing the right thing.

Even Maria had looked sceptical when Amelie had informed her where she was headed, her gaze taking in the jade-green knee-length wraparound dress made of soft cotton that emphasised Amelie's small waist and moulded her curves, the edges trimmed with the same *sankofa* kente design that labelled Atu's chalet.

She'd given her word, however. And, like with everything connected to the maddening man, doing anything other than proving she was a strong, independent woman severely chafed.

At her knock, he opened the door, and despite his being fully dressed, not shirtless as when she'd last seen him, that perfidious lust-filled sensation sped up her heartbeat again.

Every stitch of clothing, from the pristine white shirt with its sleeves folded halfway up his strong forearms, the dark trousers, to his polished hand-made shoes, shrieked bespoke sophistication.

His earthy aftershave seemed to reach out to her, intent on reminding her what it had felt like to be pressed against that prime, ruggedly male body.

He returned her gaze with a blatant scrutiny of his own that did nothing to calm her nerves. 'Come in.'

She pasted on a cool smile, her wedge heels clicking on the wooden floor as she entered, acutely aware that he followed close behind.

'Would you like a drink?'

Alcohol probably wasn't a great idea, but she needed something to calm her nerves. 'A white wine spritzer, thanks.'

As he went to the small bar at the opposite end of the chalet, the heavenly scent of sizzling prawns hit her nostrils. Moving towards the double doors, she spotted her chef, tucked away in one corner of the balcony, preparing their dinner.

Then her gaze took in the whole scene.

Wooden candelabra she'd designed herself, lit with scented candles, were positioned on a pristine white-clothed table with a kente runner, complemented by tasteful silverware.

The intimate setting made her heart lurch. Made her dwell for several dangerous moments on the secret wishes she usually refused to acknowledge in the light of day.

On the loneliness that had become a cloak she couldn't seem to shed.

'I thought we'd eat first, then get down to business,' Atu said as he returned, holding out her drink.

Her stomach gave an insistent growl just then, reminding her that she hadn't eaten since breakfast. She felt her face warm up, but all Atu did was give an almost indulgent smile as he waved her outside.

'Come. Let's not keep your chef waiting.'

Mensah, the chef, smiled when he saw her. 'Good evening, Amelie. I hope you're hungry.'

Her smile was easier. 'I'm in for a treat, I'm sure.'

She'd subsidised the skilled young chef's culinary education, and been thrilled when he'd accepted a position on her staff. He was an in-

valuable asset who kept their loyal guests returning time after time.

But for how long? What if by this time next
year she was forced to lay off some or all of her
staff, including Mensah?

'Do all your staff call you by your first name?'

She started at Atu's low, disgruntled demand.
He stood next to the table, his hands gripping the
chair he'd pulled out for her.

Her pulse kicked again, this time with shameless glee. 'What's it to you? Surely you're not
jealous?'

Shadow and lightning moved through his eyes,
reminding her that theirs was a history made of
secretive highs and grief-stricken lows. That the
illicit connection they couldn't seem to escape
had come with a steep prize.

'Let's not invite indigestion as an unwanted
third guest, shall we?'

Perhaps it was because she'd felt that same bite
of jealousy that she let him off the hook. She took
her seat, sipped her spritzer and enjoyed the glorious sunset that arrived minutes before their dinner was served.

The prawn and pawpaw salad drizzled with a
lemon dressing was superb, and she found herself
responding to the easy conversation Atu initiated,

his desire to stay away from business or personal subjects making the food go down with ease.

He declined coffee, and she refused dessert, opting for a second glass of spritzer.

She spotted the blueprints laid out on the dining table that was tucked in one corner of the living room as she followed him inside after the chef had departed, a wide smile on his face after accepting a giant tip from Atu.

Curbing a fierce urge to look closer, she dragged her attention away. Only to spot the packed weekender standing near the bedroom doorway.

'You're leaving?' she blurted, actively despising the chasm that yawned wide somewhere in her midriff.

His gaze flicked from the bag to her face. 'Is that disappointment I hear, Amelie?'

'Of course not,' she retorted briskly, despite her belly dipping alarmingly at the way he'd said her name.

His features hardened with sharp intent. 'However this meeting ends, I'm leaving at the end of it.'

She hated the way her chest clenched at those words. He was leaving. She should be celebrating. And yet not even the idea that she wouldn't need to explain his presence to her mother alleviated the curiously bereft hollow inside her.

Because her instinct warned her that while he might walk away if she persisted with her *no* at the end of this meeting, the future of her resort would still hang in the balance.

Unbidden, her gaze darted back to the blueprints.

He waved her towards them. 'Shall we...?'

She remained rooted to the spot, almost afraid to venture closer. Not because she feared she wouldn't like whatever he laid out for her, but because she was worried that she *would*.

He spotted her reluctance, his jaw tightening. 'Can you keep an open mind, just for tonight?'

'What's the point?'

A twitch rippled through his jaw. 'Nothing worth achieving in life comes without a measure of risk.'

Amelie felt herself wavering, but firmed her resolve as a memory flickered at the back of her mind. 'Yesterday you said I should accept the devil I know. What did you mean?'

That familiar shadow drifted over his face. When his jaw clenched tighter, she thought he wouldn't answer. But then, 'I'm not the only one in the Quayson Group who wants this to happen. You probably know that by now.'

Ice danced down her spine. 'You mean your father?'

His gaze didn't waver from hers. 'Yes,' he stated unequivocally.

'So what you're saying is that, no matter what I do, you and your family are coming for me?'

Impatience dragged away the shadows. 'You barely broke even at your last quarter. You need to make changes or you'll sink. Sometimes you have to make tough decisions for the greater good.'

'And you believe "the greater good" is giving you what you want and watching you walk away with the only thing that keeps my mother from falling apart?'

His nostrils thinned on a sharp inhalation. And, yes, it pleased her to see his frustration had intensified too.

Join the club.

Without answering, he strolled to the blueprints, placing his after-dinner glass of whisky next to the large sheets. For an age, he simply stared at them, and with each moment that passed, her resolve crumbled a little.

She *yearned* to see those blueprints.

'I'm willing to make a concession,' he said.

Why the hell did her heart jump at that? He was acting as if she owed him the right to make concessions, not the other way around.

'You forget that you're the one in need, not me.'

He raised his head and speared her with incisive eyes. 'I'll keep your name in whatever contract we agree between us.'

Amelie was glad she'd held her ground. 'Insult me some more, why don't you?'

His eyes narrowed. 'Is a hostile takeover really what you want? I could buy all the land around you, build another resort and overwhelm you within the year. Then buy you out for pennies on the dollar.'

The heart that had jumped a minute ago plummeted to her feet. It took everything in her not to show how alarmed she was at his threat.

'At least I'd go down fighting. History would show I didn't give in to the almighty Quaysons.'

'Maybe you would—but would it keep you warm at night?' he taunted coolly.

'Maybe not. But neither will handing everything I've worked for over to you. I'd say we're at an impasse. But I never wanted to deal with you in the first place, so...' She let her words trail off, staring him down in open challenge.

He stalked to the window, frustration in his every step. Despite the volatile atmosphere between them, she couldn't keep her eyes from following that hypnotic, leonine swagger, from watching the wide expanse of his shoulders, the gladiator-like line of his torso, tapering down to the tight clench of his buttocks, and the powerful legs that had trapped her so firmly this afternoon.

Her mouth dried and her nipples puckered in recollection of being up close against all that masculine power. All that thrilling heat and sensual promise.

With equal grace, he pivoted. Caught her unguarded gaze and stopped in his tracks.

For an age, they stared at each other, one turbulent subject momentarily abandoned in favour of another rife with equally heightened, equally disturbing power.

She held her breath as he stalked his way back to her to stand a foot from her, staring down into her upturned face as she fought to remember to breathe.

'Tell me what you want.'

The low-voiced demand was half growled, sending frissons of heat dancing over her skin.

Several requests rushed to the tip of her tongue, each one hotly discarded as inappropriate, traitorous and far too demeaning. Because, first and foremost, she wanted to feel those sensual lips on hers, those arms and hands branding her body. Then she wanted the hostilities between their families done away with. After that she wanted a thriving resort that equalled the Quayson Group.

And she could have none of them.

Because the man who could grant her all those things was the same man seeking to take away her most precious possession.

'It's just you and me here right now, Amelie. No one else.'

Her lips twisted, but he held up a hand before she could speak.

'And you have my word that I won't use whatever you say against you.'

She searched his face, wondering why her instincts weren't shrieking at her. And she realised why... She believed him.

But just in time she reminded herself that it didn't matter. Nothing mattered besides doing the right thing by her family. Which meant rejecting everything Atu stood for.

So she gave the only answer she could. 'I want nothing from you.'

CHAPTER FIVE

ATU BIT BACK a growl of frustration. His father's constant calls demanding progress were the reason he was cutting his trip short. Because unless Atu warned the old man off face to face, his father might try a different tactic altogether. One that would definitely achieve an adverse effect with Amelie. Possibly distress her even further.

He tried not to examine the flash of protectiveness that lit through him at the thought. Just as he'd tried to dismiss her heated accusations last night. And failed.

He'd walked for a solid hour after their encounter on the beach, the demons of the past dogging his footsteps and his thoughts. He'd seen no merit in admitting to Amelie that, yes, he'd known something was wrong with his brother that night. That, fresh from his latest vicious confrontation with his father, fresh from being chillingly reminded that he was second-best and was only needed as the support act for his older brother, he hadn't been in the mood to heed his instinct.

Furious with his inability to crush that knot of pain in his gut at his father's words, Atu hadn't stopped to examine whether the throwaway comments Fiifi had been making in the weeks before his twenty-fifth birthday held any weight. Hadn't wondered why his brother was drinking more than usual—why his interaction with Amelie's sister seemed a little more fraught than usual. Besides, hadn't theirs always been a hot-blooded relationship, full of angst and overblown displays of emotion? A textbook *Romeo and Juliet* relationship fuelled by the increasing tensions between their families?

He'd ignored his instinct and just about everything else the moment Amelie Hayford had sashayed up to him, her beautiful eyes wide and hungry, with that body that seemed to have accelerated from girl to woman overnight, stoking lustful flames he'd been trying to ignore for months.

He hadn't needed that particular temptation. Not on top of everything else. Not when he'd been silently condemning his own brother for obsessing over a woman who'd merely added to the frictions within the family.

Yet all it had taken was a look from her alluring eyes, the sound of her sultry voice as she'd asked if he was okay, to turn the blaze into an inferno.

And even after all this time—after tasting her

on the beach last night and this afternoon in the spa room—Atu couldn't even say definitively that he wouldn't succumb to temptation again if he could go back...

Teeth gritted, he focused on their conversation. 'When was the last time you took a vacation?' he asked, his frustration mounting higher.

Confusion wrinkled her smooth brow. 'What?'

'It's not a trick question, Amelie.'

God, why did simply uttering her name make the blood surge faster through his veins? She twisted her lips to the side, a tic he recognised meant she was measuring her words. Probably debating whether to give him a straight answer or make him work harder for it.

Why the hell did that turn him on? He inwardly shook his head. It was a good thing he was leaving. This woman came with far too much baggage, on top of the family issues already writhing between them.

'I don't remember.'

'I have a proposal for you,' he said.

Her eyes widened, then dropped to his mouth before darting away hastily.

Satisfaction eased through him. He wasn't ashamed to admit that seeing her sexual interest, no matter how quickly suppressed, pleased him.

'Not that type of proposal. But we can tackle that later if you want.'

Her eyes immediately flashed, singeing him even from across the room. 'In your dreams.'

He suppressed a smile.

The animosity she'd shown him thus far had almost convinced him he was fighting a losing battle. But her responses told a different story.

Not that he was going to use their chemistry in that way.

First he would win her business professionally. Then he would slay this particular sexual beast that had been reawakened since she'd walked into his office last week.

No. Not since last week.

Since a timid young woman—now a confident, take-charge temptress who drove him insane— had attempted a flirtation without realising the fire she was stoking. She'd been far too beguiling even back then. In the intervening years Amelie's allure had simply grown.

Remember what this woman means to your family.

He gritted his teeth and pushed that thought away. He might be undertaking this project at his father's command, but that didn't mean he wouldn't do things his own way. After all, he'd done it multiple times before—made a few billion while cloaked by his black sheep label.

But you want to earn his regard. His respect. Isn't that why you returned? To earn a crumb of the easy affection your father gave Fiifi?

The reminder chafed but, try as he might, he couldn't dismiss it. Couldn't cauterise the open wound of rejection and disregard he seemed to reap from his father simply by breathing.

'Malaysia or Malta. Take your pick,' he said, his tone harsher than he'd intended.

She started, her beautiful eyes widening. She'd edged towards the table while he'd been lost in his bitter thoughts, casting furtive glances at the blueprints.

'What are you talking about?'

He nodded to the blueprints. 'We'll visit one. Or both. You can assess the finished project for yourself. See my vision of what this place could be.'

Interest sparked in her eyes. Then frustration bit through him when he saw her eyes dim.

'No. That's out of the question.'

'Because you're afraid?'

Her plump lips pursed and heat shot through his groin.

'Excuse me?'

'I didn't stutter, Amelie. In business, you either

move forward or you die.' He shrugged. 'Some would say that applies to life too.'

A look shrouded her face. He wanted to ask what or whom she was thinking about, but he forced his mind to remain on business. For now.

It occurred to him then that he didn't know if she was involved with anyone. And that thought chafed too.

'Is it just your mother you're concerned about? Or is it someone else? A lover, perhaps?'

His breath locked in his chest as he waited for her to cycle through her outrage and give him an answer.

'Not that it's any of your business, but, no, there's no lover.' She tilted her head, eyeing him with mockery and a trace of something else he couldn't quite decipher. 'Since you think I'm capable of duplicity, I take it *you* go around kissing other women when you're involved with someone else?'

The fire in her eyes intensified the heat in his groin. Dear God, he wanted to be consumed in it. 'Is that your way of asking if *I'm* seeing anyone?'

'It's my way of warning you not to tar me with the same brush as you.'

With a start of surprise, Atu realised he was enjoying this. Her spark had ignited something within him, burning away the ennui he'd dwelt with for the last few years.

He strolled around the table, drawing closer until only a few feet separated them. He inhaled, unable to stop himself from drawing the sensual, sexy scent of her perfume into his lungs.

This was complicated, dangerous territory. But he couldn't resist. Just as he'd been unable to resist her eight years ago.

She's not offering now...

He curbed another smile. Perhaps not. But he'd always enjoyed a challenge.

'Something funny?' she snapped, her fingers tightening around her glass.

'Anyone told you you're simply alluring when you adopt that affronted minx routine?'

Her delicate jaw clenched. 'It's not a routine.'

'It is jealousy, then?' He'd experienced an unwanted taste of it, watching her smile at the chef earlier this evening. Payback was a satisfying bitch.

She blinked. Then her gaze swept away from his. He wanted to cup her chin, redirect those stunning eyes back to his.

'Can we get back to business, please?' she asked.

'I'm not seeing anyone, by the way, so you can put your claws away.'

Her lips worked, no doubt formulating a cutting response.

He turned to the blueprints, simply to avoid bending low and fusing his mouth to her far too enticing lips.

'So…which one?'

Her gaze dropped to the table and a wave of longing swept over her features, quickly extinguished as she folded her arms. 'I can't.'

He'd learned as a child, faced with the severe imbalance of affection from parents who had clearly favoured their firstborn son, that to be taken seriously he had to be assertive, to make his demands heard or be lost in chilling indifference. He'd been forced to suppress softer feelings that would only earn him ridicule from his father and pity from his mother.

Excising that trait had served him well into adulthood. More and more he reaped the benefits of it. He went after what he wanted with little regard for the consequences.

So he waited as Amelie battled with herself. She swallowed, her arms relaxing as her gaze dropped down to the table once more. 'Malaysia,' she murmured.

He nodded, curbing a wild, almost possessed need to march her to her residence, make her pack right away so they could leave.

'How long has Maria worked for you?' he asked.

Her gaze continued to linger on the blueprints as she answered, 'Almost as long as I've been in charge.'

'So she knows the workings of this place inside out?'

She started to nod, then stopped herself, frowning as his meaning sank in. 'If you're suggesting—?'

'That you take a bold step towards salvaging a sinking ship? Yes, I am.'

He expected another cutting retort, but another expression crossed her face, this one containing a haunted yearning he wanted to deny but knew only too well. It resembled the same yearning he managed to keep locked down tight. Most of the time...

'I don't know how my mother will take it.'

The faint vulnerability in her voice threatened to soften something inside him. He knew only too well what it was like to go against a parent's wishes. But wasn't the reverse why he was here?

While he was proud of the wild success he'd

achieved outside of his family's sphere of influence, he still bore the Quayson name. And, while he didn't feel the need to atone for his black sheep status, didn't he feel...something close?

His own father had threatened everything from cutting him off financially to totally disowning him eight years ago. He'd gone through with the first but, being down one heir, he'd had to rethink alienating his remaining two sons.

Amelie and her mother would see things differently a year or two from now, when he'd turned the fortunes of this resort around. Granted, it would have his family's name plastered all over it, but he had never claimed to be a saint.

His gaze fell on the plump lower lip she was worrying with her white, even teeth. His shaft swelled as memories of kissing those lips reignited, reeling out like the sharpest 3D movie, until he had to suppress a groan and lock his knees to keep from reaching for her, repeating the heady episode that had fevered his blood and interrupted his thoughts these last few hours.

No, he was far from sainthood. But he also knew now wasn't the time to give in to rampant temptation. Not when his father was making threats.

'I can have my people meet with her, if you want.'

Fierce protectiveness washed over her face. 'No. Absolutely not.'

Her reaction made him wonder whether the rumours he'd heard about Priscilla Hayford's reclusiveness were true. Whether the loss of her eldest daughter and husband had permanently broken the strong and compassionate woman she'd been before all the acrimony had set in.

And how much his own father was culpable.

He swallowed the distaste filling his mouth.

'I'll leave you to deal with your mother on your own.'

The vulnerability remained, even as that stubborn chin lifted. 'You're assuming I'm agreeing to this…'

'I haven't heard a *no* yet.' Again, he infused implacable challenge into his tone. Then he glanced pointedly at his watch. 'I have a meeting in Accra in a few hours. What's your answer, Amelie?'

Now that he'd sensed her acquiescence, the need to bind her to him rippled through him like a fever. As did the need to be free, even if for a short period, from his father's vengeful directives.

'I'll come on one condition.'

He neutralised his features, dead set on not showing an ounce of the emotion roiling through him. Emotion he deciphered as thick, unrelenting *anticipation*.

'I'm listening.'

'If I'm not convinced by what you show me in Malaysia, you'll leave me alone.'

The thought of walking away from her—for any reason—triggered a negative reaction in him. While he was convinced visiting his resort would change her mind, her condition wasn't one he was going to accept.

He refused to ask himself why he felt so strongly about it, and knew his rejection of it stemmed from a place he didn't want to examine.

'No, I don't need to grant that condition. You'll come. You'll like what you see. And you'll accept my terms.'

Her jaw slackened for a moment before she caught herself. 'Your arrogance truly knows no bounds, does it?'

He allowed himself a small smile of satisfaction, which swiftly turned to clawing hunger when she gave a small gasp and her gaze dropped to his mouth.

'No, it doesn't. And you'll be glad for it when you reap the rewards from giving me what I want.'

* * *

Amelie sipped the perfectly chilled vintage champagne just served to her by an impeccably dressed flight attendant, fervently willing her hand to stop shaking and her head to stop reeling.

The drink went down smoothly, but it did nothing to calm her nerves.

She wasn't sure what surprised and disturbed her most—the fact that she'd gathered the courage to pack her suitcase, climb into the back of the sleek and shiny town car Atu had sent to Salt-pond this morning to bring her to Accra, or the fact that she'd done it despite the distressing row with her mother last night, once she'd made up her mind to go ahead with this.

Her soul shrivelled in recollection of her parent's reaction to the news that she was accompanying Atu Quayson to Malaysia and considering his offer to subsume their resort.

Her mother's look of utter devastation had passed quickly, to be replaced by disappointment, then fury at what she'd stated was Amelie's failure to keep 'that evil family' away from her beloved legacy.

'They're threatening to take over with or without our co-operation, Maa,' she'd pleaded. 'I need time to find a way out.'

'And your way of finding time is to fly off with the Quayson boy?' she'd replied scathingly, her grief-filled eyes darkening with disappointed fury. 'You are a Hayford. I expect you to tell them we will never co-operate. But, no. You have been seen accommodating him in our resort instead,' she'd accused hoarsely.

Amelie gasped. 'You knew?'

'Of course I knew. Just because I'm not involved in the day-to-day running of the place, it doesn't mean I don't take an interest in what's happening here. It's all we have left after those people took everything away from us!'

'But you never talk to me about it. You don't even…' She'd bitten her tongue, reluctant to admit how she truly felt about her mother cloistering herself in the master suite day after day, only emerging occasionally, cloaked in grief and with a faraway look that said she didn't care about the present or her remaining daughter, only the past and the husband and child she'd lost in quick succession.

'I don't even what? Hold your hand and tell you every day what a good job you're doing?'

Every cell in her body had yearned to scream *Yes!*—to regress to being a needy child seeking acceptance and affection from a parent. She'd wanted to demand why that was too much to ask. But she'd feared the answer. Feared her mother might tell her she didn't merit the same love her sister had so easily been granted. That the endless stream of devotion she'd showered upon her older sister and her husband was long depleted. Or, worse, that any remaining reserves she could dredge up would only go to sustain the memory of her firstborn and never be extended to her remaining living child.

Amelie hadn't wanted to be reminded that, despite her parents adoring their firstborn daughter, they'd fervently wished their second child to be a son. They'd never got over their disappointment when their wish hadn't been granted.

She'd pushed the stark reminder to the back of her mind as her mother had condemned her for her decisions.

'How do you know he's not simply getting you out of the way so his father or brother can take over anyway?'

For some reason her insides had tightened at this indictment against Atu. She'd found herself defending him. The man she'd kissed not once but twice, when she should be staying far away from him.

'Because if he really wanted that he could've

done it from the comfort of his office back in Accra. He didn't have to come here and talk to me.'

And then she'd realised she believed it. Perhaps it was foolish, but she didn't hate Atu's stance in coming to the resort to face her, instead of leaving it to his team of cut-throat lawyers and business executives.

Her mother's eyes had narrowed then. 'Sweet heaven, you sound as if you're defending him.'

She'd ignored the traitorous heat climbing into her face. 'I'm not. But if you've been keeping an eye on things, then you know we're barely hanging on. Would you prefer to do nothing at all? I don't have any other choice, Maa.'

'Your father would've found a way,' she'd muttered then, her face clouding over before she'd turned away from Amelie, shutting her out with the same finality with which she'd been shutting her out for years.

Amelie had been alternately grateful that her mother hadn't seen the pain coursing through her and angry with herself for the immediate instinct to suppress that pain, to bear it in silence so her mother wouldn't suffer further.

Perhaps because she'd been worn down, she'd found herself beginning to look forward to leaving the resort behind for a while—even if it was with Atu.

And then a different sort of emotion had struck. One she was still trying to suppress.

It was the quiet fizz of excitement, bubbling just beneath her skin. It had grown audaciously when she'd met with Maria, to temporarily hand over the reins of her beloved resort.

When Maria's scepticism had given way to supportive understanding, Amelie had had to blink back tears. If nothing else, she knew her resort would remain in competent hands while she was away.

So now here she was, after being whisked through VIP Customs at Accra's Kotoka International Airport, then driven across the baking tarmac to a gleaming cream private jet with gold trimmings and the 'Q' logo exhibited boldly on its tail fin. Minutes later, she'd been ensconced on the Quaysons' jaw-dropping, extremely luxurious private jet, waiting for the man himself before they took off for Kuala Lumpur, via a quick refuelling stop in Dubai.

A small crew consisting of two pilots and four attendants had greeted her, then informed her that Mr Quayson would be arriving shortly.

She took another sip of champagne, enjoying

the taste in spite of giving up on the drink doing anything to calm her nerves. She doubted anything would, but perhaps during this time away she would find a solution to her problem that didn't involve extending her mother's pain and misery.

She was still busy ignoring the sceptical voice taunting her that pigs might fly before that happened when she looked up to see Atu striding down the aisle towards her.

Dear God, he had no right to look this good. Had no right to interfere with her heart's rhythm the way he so effortlessly did just by existing. She tried not to ogle the sight he made in a torso-moulding polo shirt and cargo pants…how each movement of his body reeked of utter confidence.

When he stopped beside her, fixing his far too vivid gaze on her, she wanted to rail at the fates for the breathless fever raging in her pelvis.

'Your journey from Saltpond was fine, I hope?' he enquired, his voice low, deep, and devastating to her equilibrium.

She cleared her throat and attempted a light, casual tone. 'Yes, thanks.'

'What's wrong? And don't tell me it's nothing.' She knew he was seeing the same shadows and weariness she'd spotted in her bathroom mirror this morning.

'My mother didn't take the news well.'

He remained silent for a moment before his nostrils flared. 'And yet you still came.'

There was speculation in his voice, along with a note she couldn't quite decipher, and it sent tingles down her spine.

She shook her head. 'I don't want to talk about my mother. Or our families.'

He studied her for several more seconds. Then he summoned an attendant. When she hurried over, an eager smile on her face, Atu nodded towards Amelie's glass. 'I'll have the same, thanks,' he said, without taking his gaze off Amelie's face.

She wasn't sure why her breath snagged in her throat as they waited for all of ten seconds before his drink was delivered.

Around them, the crew were readying for take-off. The doors were sealed; the pilots had disappeared into the cockpit. But all she could focus on was Atu leaning forward, his broad shoulders filling her vision and his fresh citrusy aftershave playing havoc with her senses.

'I have two proposals for you,' he told her.

Her mirthless laughter seared her throat. 'I'm

still on the fence about the wisdom of the last one I agreed to.'

He shrugged, drawing her attention to the latent power in his broad shoulders, to the reality that he only needed to be within touching distance to make her feel shamefully breathless.

'This one might cause a little less stress. Perhaps even alleviate it.'

The plane gave a small jolt as it left the hangar. A drop of champagne spilled from her glass onto her fingers. She raised her hand and licked the droplet, then inhaled sharply when he gave a low growl.

The resulting punch of feminine power made her smile confidently. 'Let's hear it, then…'

He seemed to be having trouble focusing on their conversation, and Amelie couldn't help the flash of excitement that lit up in her belly.

'I want to call a truce. No dredging up our history unless we both want to discuss it.'

Which left business—and the remaining subject that had occupied her mind for far too long. The one seeming to loom even larger than the elephant in the room that was their family feud.

Even other peripheral subjects, like how exactly he'd earned the 'black sheep' label, felt secondary to the live wire of the chemistry writhing between them.

It was a charged subject that he wasn't going to place on the back burner of his 'truce' proposal, judging by the fierce intensity in his eyes, the way his gaze kept raking her face, lingering at the pulse beating in her throat...

'You said two. What's the other?' she asked as the plane rumbled onto the runway.

It gathered speed, as did the urgency of Atu's regard. She dragged her gaze from his, glanced out of the small porthole at the buildings flashing by. Soon they would be airborne, winging away from the responsibility and heartache she'd been consumed with since her sister, and then her father, had passed away.

Since continuing the family legacy had become her only focus.

Her shoulders lost a touch of their tenseness, and the tightness at her temples she'd learned to live with eased as the plane gained speed.

Then his fingers brushed over the back of her hand, willing her focus back to him. The stark need in his face made her breath feel strangled in her throat.

'I want you in my bed. I want you underneath

me. I want… I *need* to know what it feels like to possess you,' he rasped.

'*This isn't going away…*'

His words from the beach resonated within her.

'If I take you up on your…proposal…it'll be on my terms. You may have got me here by taking away most of my choices, but this won't be one of them.'

She saw his untrammelled need to dominate her in this too. A need she suspected had been branded into his DNA. He was the alpha male, intent on having his way in all things.

But she boldly held his gaze, the urge not to let her own need defeat her into submitting surging furiously inside her.

The ripple in his jaw told her he was displeased, but then a flash of admiration gleamed in his eyes.

Still, she held her breath, until he lifted his glass, not quite touching it to hers, but not acquiescing either.

'I reserve the right *not* to make it easy for you to prolong it. That's my best and final offer.'

Maybe it was her sense of freedom, the relief that accompanied leaving her troubles behind if only for a short time, that made her lean forward.

'Challenge accepted,' she said, and touched her

glass to his just as the wheels of the plane left *terra firma.*

She took another sip of her drink and together they watched the city fall away beneath them. She only turned her attention back to him when the jet broke through the clouds. And only as she watched his own shoulders drop did it register that he'd been tense too.

As if he too had needed the escape.

But surely not?

He and his family ruled the city beneath them. Between the goldmines and the luxury hotels and the numerous banking interests, they'd been elevated to an eye-wateringly wealthy status decades ago.

Amelie secretly suspected that, while the two men had once been friends, it had been her father's obsession with keeping up with the Quaysons and ultimately failing that had contributed to the initial rift. The tragedy of losing their eldest children in the same accident had been the straw that had finally broken the camel's back.

She glanced at Atu now from beneath her eyelashes, watching him sprawl in his seat, effortlessly drawing her attention to his body.

He locked his eyes on her before she could look away.

She opened her mouth, then realised she didn't want to talk business—and talking about sex was way too risky, considering how she was feeling.

Which left her with nothing to say and an ever-increasing desire to give in to his *sooner rather than later* time frame.

Clearly deciphering her dilemma, he let loose a conceited smile as he watched her. 'Don't tell me your little condition is already causing you problems?' he drawled with wry amusement.

'Not at all. I was wondering why you came back to Ghana, considering you've set the hotel world alight in Asia and Europe,' she blurted, plucking the subject out of the air.

Humour evaporated from his face. 'I believe that falls under one of our no-go areas.'

She swallowed at the hard bite to his words. Then she felt a weird little sense of kinship with him, because she suspected his reasons were familial and as strained as hers were.

'Why aren't you seeing anyone?' he parried.

It was her turn to be unnerved. 'Excuse me?'

'After going to great lengths to state your stance on fidelity, I'm wondering why a beautiful woman like you is single. It can't be for lack of male attention.'

'No, it's not. It's by choice.'

There was no need to tell him she hadn't felt like dating recently. That the spark he evoked so effortlessly in her was totally missing with every other man she'd met in the last few years.

Something flickered in his eyes—a flare of possession and intent that made her body prickle alternately with heat and cold. But she didn't have to dwell on it because he'd reached into his brief-case and taken out a thick brochure. Although the heading stated it was a guest activity list for the Q Cove Resort, there were no pictures, just glossy text.

'I know you've seen the blueprints, but I want you to see the finished product first-hand. Make a list of what you'd like to experience while we're there.' He slid it across to her, then rose. 'I have a few calls to make. I'll see you in a few hours.'

Amelie watched him leave with a sense of loss—a feeling she was starting to associate with watching Atu walk away from her.

It struck here then that now he'd got his way, and she'd agreed to hear him out, she'd expected him to press his advantage at the first opportunity. But she should've known that he'd do the opposite. After all, she'd handed herself over to him for the next two weeks.

Had he grown bored? Like a predator with its prey finally within its grasp?

She grimaced, irritated by using that unfavourable description.

She was no one's prey!

So why was she feeling at odds because he'd left her so soon? Bereft, even?

Exasperated with herself, she flicked through the brochure, her eyes widening at the extensive range of sustainable services Atu's resort provided. A man-made, rain-fed lake delivered water and electricity to the whole resort, making it completely self-reliant. A high percentage of the resort's food was grown on-site or sourced through local merchants. It had achieved an industrial level of recycling that made her own previously held belief that her resort was sustainable a laughable joke.

Every stitch of fabric used at his resort was sustainable—including the staff's clothing. Guests were encouraged to use the on-site couturier for the duration of their stay and donate their clothes to charity before departure, and the subtle encouragement to travel light and reduce their carbon footprint had worked wonders.

She read through it twice, fighting twinges of jealousy. Grabbing a pen, she ticked several random boxes, assuring herself that it wouldn't live up to her expectations.

Atu returned just before they landed to refuel in Dubai. Expecting more of that sexual intensity from him, she was again nonplussed when he went into flawless host mode.

'The attendants will be along with some refreshments. Lunch will be in fifteen minutes.'

They ate in companionable silence, and then he sat back after their meal was done and they'd taken off again. 'I have a few more items to take care of. There's a bedroom in the back if you want to rest.'

She followed his gaze to the door at the rear of the plane, then immediately felt light-headed as sensual images bombarded her. All she needed to do was say the word and she would experience the full, mind-melting magic he'd already given her a taste of.

She squirmed as heat spiked through her.

Was she really built for casual sex?

Or was she overthinking everything?

Theirs would be a mutually agreed-upon casual fling. Not like the melodramatic one Esi had had with Atu's brother. There would be no emotions and therefore no heartache—

'Amelie?'

'Hmm?' She glanced up at him.

His gaze was filled with amusement and heat as he waved a hand at the brochure. 'I asked if you'd chosen.'

'I…um… Yes.'

He picked up the brochure. 'Spear fishing, wind-sailing *and* abseiling? Very brave for the girl I remember, who was afraid to even venture near the swimming pool until I coaxed you into it. Are you sure you don't want to add bungee jumping to your list, just to make it a total adrenaline junkie's experience?'

Her eyes widened in mild shock—both at the activities she'd so carelessly picked and at the fact that he remembered those long-forgotten times. She had indeed had an initial fear of swimming in the big children's pool. All it had taken was one of Atu's rare smiles and his cocky teasing to make her take the plunge.

But those idyllic days were far behind her.

'I'm sure. And, in case you haven't noticed, I'm not that girl any more.'

Something dark and thrilling flashed in his eyes. 'I've noticed,' he replied, with an intensity that sat heavily between them.

When she ventured a look at him, she caught a shaft of pain in his eyes, quickly disguised as he picked up his glass of wine. Again, questions brimmed on the tip of her tongue, but, reminded of their agreement, she bit them back. Or at least she tried to.

The words that spilled from her lips were the last she'd expected. 'What's your reason for being unattached?'

His eyebrows rose.

'What?' she demanded, even as her inner voice asked her what she was doing. 'You can ask me, but I can't ask you?'

His lips twisted and his lashes veiled the look in his eyes. When they rose again, she gasped at the unabashed hunger in his eyes. 'Because I like a challenge, and they've become thin on the ground recently...'

The unspoken *until now* trumpeted loudly between them.

She wanted to snap that she wasn't a recreational diversion for him to pass the time with. But wasn't that essentially what they'd agreed? A tryst while they were away from the condemning eyes of their families to dissipate this chemistry between them?

And, deep down, didn't going toe to toe with him make her senses sing?

Beware of the dangerous road you're taking...

'Be careful you don't go from boredom to being completely out of your depth,' she told him.

He threw back his head and laughed, and Amelie was struck dumb by the transformation of his face.

In an instant she was transported back to being a wide-eyed teenager, watching Atu Quayson charm every female within a square mile with his insanely gorgeous smile, feeling her heart crash about in her chest before swan-diving into her belly.

It made her literally hold her breath, and she felt almost mournful when it disappeared, like a spectacular mirage, always destined to be a wonderful but fleeting thing.

True enough, he sobered up quickly. 'I'd consider myself well-warned, but I doubt the caution is necessary.'

'Why not?'

The eyes that met hers were cool and jaded. 'Because I'm yet to meet a woman who under-promises and over-delivers. One who doesn't have a hidden agenda buried beneath false charm, superficial beauty or overblown emotions.'

For some reason his answer twisted something inside her, making her clutch her glass tighter. 'How utterly appalling for you,' she said, gleeful when her words emerged as dryly as she'd intended them. 'So you've given up the search for your one true love?'

Instead of the sardonicism she'd expected, his face assumed a granite harshness that made her belly flip over.

'True love?' he echoed with searing bitterness. 'So-called true love killed my brother and your sister, Amelie. I'd be careful how you throw about those meaningless words. People pay for them not just with their own lives but with the scarred lives they leave behind.'

Her mouth gaped in shock as he surged to his feet and strode away from her without a backward glance.

CHAPTER SIX

ATU SLAMMED THE meeting compartment door with more force than necessary, seething more at himself than at the woman he'd marched away from.

Granted, he'd had a stronger reaction to Amelie's words than he'd expected. It had been years, after all, since anyone had dared to utter those two words in his presence.

Hell, before this week he'd resisted every effort to be drawn into conversation about the brother he'd held in such high regard and lost. Just as he'd resisted discussing the reasons behind Fiifi's erratic behaviour just before his death until Amelie had brought it up on the beach.

True love... Romeo and Juliet...

He wasn't sure when he'd grown to despise those words with such vehement force.

Perhaps it had been when his older brother had announced to him—in confidence—that he intended to walk away from the family. To give it all up in the name of love.

Atu had pleaded with him to reconsider. Because even then he'd known that he wouldn't be considered an adequate replacement. That, should his brother leave, purportedly to pursue an acrimony-free life with Esi Hayford, the stark indifference he'd inspired in his father would be made more acute.

Or perhaps it was when he'd watched Fiifi make a fool over himself over a woman who, despite her clear feelings for his brother, had wanted him to jump through a thousand hoops, playing games that had driven his brother insane with jealousy and rage, triggering the recklessness that had eventually taken his life.

All in the name of *true love*…

Even before the weekend his brother and Amelie's sister had perished, he'd known that emotions were inconveniences to be placed at arm's length…further even, if one could help it.

Worse still, they were a sharp tool wielded by the cruel.

Like his father.

Joseph Quayson was fond of publicly proclaiming to love all his sons equally, but Atu had known it was a lie long before he'd grown out of short trousers. Behind closed doors, Atu and his younger brother, Ekow, had always been made unequivocally aware that they were the second and third acts to their brother's illustrious existence. Fiifi was the chosen son and they were the spares, created to prop up his pedestal.

As much as it had grated, even then Atu had chosen to believe that if he toed the line some crumbs of affection might drop his way. That his father would acknowledge and perhaps even respect him as a rule-follower...someone he could trust to be a solid second.

But the dearth of his father's regard and his own mounting disinclination to be anyone's second had gradually created fractures, scarring his relationship with his father long before that fateful weekend and its aftermath, which had started the pressure for him to step into his dead brother's shoes.

And all that had been besides his father's indiscretions, the clear evidence that his parents' union had been built on lies and convenience for the sake of appearances.

His lips twisted.

True love didn't exist except in the minds of those who wanted to make excuses for their outrageous behaviour.

It was why he'd vowed long before he'd reached adulthood not to encumber himself with relationships. Mutually beneficial liaisons were enough for him. Or at least they'd been enough until they'd grown stale and left him jaded.

Wasn't it, therefore, the height of irony that he'd allowed himself to be talked into returning home because of...*emotions*?

His mother's tearful pleas for him to return. His father's stern demands from what doctors had cautioned was most likely his deathbed that he did not disgrace the family further by refusing to do the right thing. Even Ekow had weighed in, and the strain in his younger brother's voice had told him he was at breaking point.

Atu hadn't had the heart to correct his father when he'd played the emotional blackmail card and insisted that it was what his dead brother would've wanted. So he'd returned...despite the twisting in his gut as he questioned whether he'd done the right thing.

Pacing his plane's meeting area now, he let out a low, frustrated growl as the release of tension he'd experienced when the plane took off came crowding back. He strolled to one window, braced his hand above it and stared unseeing at a cluster of cumulus clouds before casting a glance at the door.

Of all the women in the world, Amelie Hayford had to be the one to burrow this deep beneath his skin, frustrating him, dredging up memories he didn't want to unearth and, yes, a passion the likes of which he'd never experienced.

He'd left the ball in her court.

But now he was glad he'd stated upfront that he would not be making it easy.

Because he needed to free himself of this *insanity*.

He needed to be free of every last Hayford, once and for all.

Slapping his hand on the polished surface above the window, he straightened, ignoring the acidic churning in his stomach that mocked his last thought.

One way or another he would conquer this fever. Perhaps even dislodge this cloud of guilt hanging over him for not being there for Fiifi in his last hours.

And in so doing he would break this bewildering hold Amelie had on him.

The Q Cove Hotel was a dream.

It was almost as if Atu had reached inside her most treasured fantasy of the perfect resort and recreated it, brick by brick, in real life. It was a vision in white set on a flat quarter-mile pristine expanse along the Desaru Coast in the eastern corner of Malaysia.

The whole resort backed on to a verdant tropical jungle.

It was breathtaking—especially seen from the comfort of the sleek helicopter that had transported them from the airport in Kuala Lumpur. Compared to her resort, Q Cove was miles away in size and luxury.

'Everything you see here will work just as well back at your resort. And with the ocean on your doorstep, it'll thrive just as well, if not more,' he said.

But Amelie was only half listening, her thoughts occupied with the changes in him.

He'd emerged from the meeting area twenty minutes before they'd landed as if their terse exchange before he'd stormed off hadn't even happened.

Instead, he'd turned on the charm offensive.

She wasn't entirely sure how to take it. On the one hand, she felt a stark need to know what he'd meant by his statement. More importantly, *who* he'd meant. Because someone had sown the seeds of those beliefs in him. And somehow he'd indicted her sister in whatever was behind his storm of words.

She'd fought the urge to go after him on the plane, to demand an explanation. Instinct had warned her to stay away. Because wasn't there a grain of truth in what he'd said? As a child, she'd believed her mother loved her enough to sustain whatever pain or strife life threw at them. But what should've been undying love had withered away under the strain of grief.

Was that true familial love? Or had she lived with an illusion before the scales were pulled from her eyes? Was it love if it could fade so quickly?

In contrast, though, she knew Esi had loved Atu's brother. Granted, it had been a melodramatic kind of love, involving copious tears interspersed with bouts of delirium, making Amelie's heart swell in awe and alarm at the grandeur of her sister's love for the firstborn Quayson.

She'd suspected saying that to Atu wouldn't go down well, so she'd retreated to the bedroom suite and attempted to rest, only to be confronted with a whole set of niggles that had meant sleep was out of the question.

The bedroom had been just as tastefully and luxuriously appointed as the rest of the jet, but it had been impossible for her to relax knowing that at some point Atu had slept on this same bed, probably with a woman…

She'd jackknifed up in bed then, unsure whether to be disappointed or afraid at the direction of her thoughts as she'd hastily returned to her seat, her thoughts in even deeper turmoil.

She glanced at him now as the helicopter settled down on the designated helipad, reminding herself that the end goal for him in all of this was to get his hands on her family's property.

The rotor blades were still spinning when he stepped down and held out his hand.

Because the resort was on the coast, the rich salty tang of the ocean blended perfectly with the dense lushness of the jungle, evoking the sensation that she was breathing in nature itself.

'Welcome to Q Cove.'

She slid her hand into his, fully expecting—and receiving—a sizzle of electric heat at the point of contact. Alongside that, she already felt mounting trepidation. That moment on the jet might have passed for him, but now she knew where he stood on emotional entanglements, she couldn't dismiss the peculiar bubble of dismay inside her.

She pressed her lips together as a trio of staff approached them.

'Welcome back, Mr Quayson.' A man in his late thirties greeted them.

Atu nodded and introduced him with a brisk smile. 'My resort director, Irfan, and his assistants, Nur and Michelle. This is Amelie. She'll be staying with me at the villa while we're here.'

She exchanged greetings with them, even as her senses flared to full alert at Atu's words. When Irfan and his team waved them towards the battery-operated buggies that waited nearby, she glanced at Atu.

'I thought I'd be staying at the resort in a hotel room?'

He caught her wrist in a loose hold and directed her towards the first buggy. 'We didn't discuss your sleeping arrangements, but I should've mentioned that this resort is fully booked all year round. There's a seven-month waiting list.'

Her eyes widened. 'Seriously?'

One corner of his mouth lifted. 'Feel free to double-check with Irfan if you don't believe me.'

'So why is this villa unoccupied?'

'Because it's my personal property. No one stays there but me. And if you're worried that you'll find yourself in a clichéd one-bed situation, just so I can have my way with you, don't be.'

Why did that both irritate and disappoint her?

She shook her head. 'What's that supposed to mean?'

His head tilted arrogantly. 'You'll see.'

With an audience within earshot, she had no choice but to curb all her questions and take a seat in the buggy. Irfan joined them, while Michelle and Nur stayed to supervise the unloading of their luggage.

'Would you like a tour now or after you've rested, Miss Hayford?' Irfan asked.

As much as she was dying to explore everything she'd seen from the air up close, she was aware her eyes felt gritty and her skin a touch grimy. Travelling for almost eighteen hours, even in jaw-dropping luxury, didn't necessarily equate to restfulness—as she'd discovered first-hand.

Plus, she didn't think she could concentrate until she knew what Atu meant by her 'sleeping arrangements'.

She saw him slide her a glance just as she opened her mouth, and he answered before she could. 'The tour can wait until later, Irfan. I'm sure Miss Hayford would like to rest after we've had some refreshments.'

Irfan nodded deferentially. 'Of course, sir. I've arranged for a light meal to be delivered shortly.

I've also put the staff on notice for any activities you would like to partake in.'

They were approaching a flat-roofed building with greenery peeking out from the top. Smartly dressed smiling staff moved with brisk efficiency, serving the few guests who milled about what appeared to be a sun-dappled reception area.

'Will there be anything else?' Irfan asked as he stepped out.

'That will be all for now, thank you.'

Amelie gazed about her with mounting interest. 'It's green everywhere,' she murmured, then realised she'd spoken aloud.

Atu nodded. 'Every guest suite was constructed either beneath a tree or with a living garden on its roof to encourage interaction with wildlife.'

Looking closer, she realised that the wood she'd thought was white from the helicopter was really a pale gold, almost matching the grains of golden sand on the beach.

She noticed that the suites grew larger and were set further apart the further they went. Then her breath caught as she spotted the structure Atu was heading towards.

The villa was magnificent.

Constructed between two large arching acacia trees, with half of its frontage wrapped in lush laburnum climbers, it blended into the forest effortlessly, and yet it owned its jaw-dropping presence.

Wide glass windows reflected the greenery and the pale wood cladding, and a wide stone-paved path connected straight down to the beach in one stunning flawless sequence of forest and beach that was simply breathtaking.

He stopped in front of a wide carved teak door, with a discreet gold plaque beside it that labelled it *Q Rainforest Suite*.

'My God, it's beautiful...' She didn't realise the soft, awed words had slipped out until he slanted her a steady glance.

'Yes. It is,' he responded simply.

He parked the buggy, stepped out and held out his hand to her.

Inside, the cool interior soothed her senses. Large, expensive tiles echoed with her footsteps, and tasteful local art provided punches of colour throughout.

Atu led her through to the living room and she stopped in awe. The walls were made entirely of glass, providing perfect staging for the rainforest that gave the villa its name.

He pressed a button and one section of the glass slid smoothly away.

The burst of birdsong was magical, accompanied occasionally by another sound she didn't immediately recognise.

'What's that?'

'We have a few families of silvered langur monkeys in the forest. If you're lucky, you might spot them while we're here.'

Slightly overcome by the sheer beauty of her surroundings, Amelie closed her eyes, lifting her face to bask in the dappled sunlight streaming in through the branches and leaves overhead.

She sensed his scrutiny and, almost compelled, opened her eyes to find his gaze fixed firmly on her.

Each room was as entrancing as the last, but it was the location of the bedroom he led her to that floored her. The glass-windowed theme had continued throughout, and the sight of the jade-tiled hot tub and adjoining small pool steps from the bedroom suite made her jaw drop. And in the middle of the pool was a smaller bed, complete with white fluffy pillows and white sheets.

It was a heavenly invitation to sleep under the stars serenaded by the sounds of nature.

The idea that she might recreate something equally enchanting at Saltpond made her yearn to blurt out that, *yes*, she would partner with him.

But then it wouldn't be a true partnership. He would be her boss. The one she answered to on a daily basis. He would be in her life for the foreseeable future... unless she chose to walk away.

Unless she let her family down...

But then hadn't she already done that in her mother's eyes?

'What's wrong?' he demanded, with an edge in his voice.

Again, a need to keep the peace made her shake her head. 'Nothing that won't work itself out eventually,' she stated archly.

He eyed her silently, then nodded.

The rest of their tour took in a state-of-the-art kitchen, a rooftop garden, another, larger swimming pool, and countless seats positioned perfectly around the villa from which to enjoy the bounteous nature all around.

The arrival of their refreshments was timed perfectly with the end of the tour. Amelie sank into an overstuffed seat in the living room and accepted a glass of fruit punch from the smiling staff member, who then turned to Atu.

'Sir, Irfan wants me to let you know that he can arrange for Assan to come by, if you want?'

For some reason his face tightened. 'No, that won't be necessary.'

She nodded and left, and Amelie glanced at him. 'Who's Assan?'

The frown didn't totally leave his face as he answered. 'He's a top masseur I poached from another resort eighteen months ago. He's in high demand in the resort...normally booked weeks in advance. But he makes time for me when I'm here.'

'And you don't want him to come because...?'

His gaze swept down for a few beats before lifting and spearing hers. 'If anyone's going to charm you with the wonders this place provides, it's going to be me.' He smiled drolly at her shocked expression. 'Does that make me sound primitive?'

'I... Yes,' she responded honestly.

He shrugged away the indictment. 'So be it.'

And that was the end of it.

Simply because she was unnerved and secretly thrilled by that raw statement, Amelie also chose to leave it alone.

They enjoyed their refreshments for a few minutes before she chanced another glance at him. His gaze was on the pool, and there was a curiously relaxed expression on his face. She'd sensed the tension leave his body as they took off from

Accra, but this was something more. Something deeper.

It resembled the same sensation she felt when she'd had a particularly great day at her resort.

'This place means something to you,' she said.

His face remained serious, but he shrugged. 'It was the very first thing I built from the ground up on my own. I'm not ashamed to admit it's a source of pride.'

She stemmed the twinge of envy and took another sip of her drink. 'How long did all this take?'

'Two years of hard work.'

There was a tight tone in his voice that jangled her nerves. 'Just hard work?'

A bitter smile twitched at his lips. 'The challenge of striking out on my own while fighting my father's influence gave it an extra edge.'

Amelie tensed. It wasn't the first time he'd hinted at being at variance with his father. And certainly going against the domineering Joseph Quayson's wishes had partly contributed to his 'black sheep' label. But when it came right down to it, she'd always believed family and legacy came first for him. Was she wrong?

'He wasn't on board with you doing this?'

A tic throbbed at his temple, but he continued

to gaze at a dragonfly flitting over the gently un-dulating water of the pool. 'If his not being "on board" with me relocating to the other side of the world meant throwing as many obstacles in my way as he could, then no. He wasn't.'

'But you did it anyway?'

Amelie realised she was leaning towards him, something inside her straining for his answer. She wasn't looking for validation so she could take the same route with her mother. Was she?

For the briefest moment Amelie caught the hint of bleakness in his eyes. An instant later it was gone.

'I'm the black sheep, remember?' His wry tone held a hint of bitterness.

'Yes, I remember. But some would say you took the negative connotations of that and made it into something better.'

She knew that not once in the midst of all his disagreements with his father had he brought his family name into disrepute.

Despite the shadows circling in his eyes, he lifted one brow sardonically. 'Is that admiration I hear in your voice?'

She shrugged, unwilling to admit that, yes, it was. And perhaps a little bit of envy. Because he'd done what she'd been unable to do—stepped out from beneath a sibling's imposingly large shadow to succeed in the face of formidable odds.

'Maybe your father felt it too. Maybe that's why he was against you leaving?' she said.

'Or maybe he just wanted me to be something I'm not,' he rasped.

'That sounds familiar,' she muttered, and then her stomach dropped when she realised she'd spoken out loud.

Circumspect eyes locked on hers. 'Your sister?'

This time her shrug was leaden, the earlier conversation with her mother echoing in her head. The urge to clam up, protect the vulnerable heart that still wanted her parent's affection and regard, burned fiercely. And yet she still found herself responding.

'Losing her was devastating for my parents. For me. But I never thought—' The lump in her throat stopped her.

Atu leaned forward. 'Never thought what?'

The demand was low-voiced…gentle, even.

She curled her fingers tighter around her glass. 'That it would devastate them so much they'd close themselves off to…everything else.'

'Not to everything else. To you. They acted like they didn't have another child. One who was living and breathing and required care and acknowledgement.'

The certainty in his voice said he knew what she meant. Perhaps even *felt* it. Had *lived* it.

For a charged span of time, neither of them spoke. Their powerful connection of empathy felt almost seismic. He was her enemy. They should have nothing in common. She shouldn't feel this swell of emotion for what he'd suffered. What they'd both suffered.

And yet...

'Have we actually discovered common ground on something?' she asked, with a laugh meant to alleviate the gravity of the realisation.

He tensed at her words, and a flash of bewilderment darted over his face before Amelie sensed his withdrawal.

'Maybe not entirely. My "black sheep" label has served me well, while you've done the opposite—attempting to fit into a mould for the sake of pleasing your mother.'

Fresh from empathising, she felt hurt prickle in her chest. Suspecting he was saying this just to distance himself from their shared experience didn't alleviate the feeling.

'So you want me to become a rebel?' she asked.

'The strongest steel is forged in the hottest

flame,' he replied cryptically, with a few more shadows darkening his eyes.

When he knocked back the rest of his drink and stood, she knew the subject was closed.

The late-afternoon sun lingered on his face, making her breath catch at the sheer perfection of his dark skin and the sensual lines of those lips she secretly yearned to savour again. The punch of hunger low in her belly made her avert her gaze before she gave herself away.

'Did you get much rest on the plane?' he asked.

The change of subject further threw her. 'Not as much as I'd have liked.'

'I'll leave you to rest, then. You'll find the senior staff's numbers next to the phone in your bedroom. If you need anything, call one of them.'

She looked up in surprise. 'You're leaving?'

'I have an engagement in Kuala Lumpur. I'm not sure how long it'll go on for. If I don't see you tonight, I'll see you at some point tomorrow.'

Her heart lurched with something cuttingly close to disappointment. What kind of appointment did he have? Was it with a woman? Despite declaring that he wanted her in his bed, he'd never assured her of exclusivity. He was an extremely eligible bachelor with a selection of drop-dead gorgeous women at his beck and call.

Mood dimmed, she set her cocktail down. 'Have a safe trip. I'm sure I'll be perfectly fine,' she replied crisply, despite the squeezing in her chest.

He frowned, as if that wasn't the answer he'd wanted to hear. Then, with a curt nod, he turned and walked away.

She stayed outside, wondering if the sun had dipped or if her plummeting mood was responsible for the sudden chill she felt.

CHAPTER SEVEN

ATU DIDN'T RETURN to the villa.

Amelie knew because she'd crashed just before sunset, with jet lag hitting her hard enough so she'd barely got through dinner and a shower before sliding gratefully between the sheets. Only to wake up just after one a.m.

She'd known she should attempt to regulate her sleep patterns, but she'd risen anyway, with a biting need driving her into walking through the villa.

She'd pulled herself up short when she'd stood on the threshold of what was evidently the master bedroom, where the impeccably made, patently un-slept-in bed had made that unsettling feeling in her midriff return full-force.

What the hell was wrong with her? Wandering around Atu Quayson's villa unnerved by the fact that she missed him?

The thought had sent her scurrying to bed, where she'd suffered restless sleep until the early hours.

Now she'd risen with a determination to do what she'd come here to do. Explore every facet of what had made the Q Cove Hotel elevate itself above being a mere resort. She might not have a rainforest to tempt guests to Saltpond, but she had the ocean, the culture and the personal touch.

Whether Atu intended to get involved or not shouldn't matter. In fact, he could stay in Kuala Lumpur for as long as he pleased.

After a dip in her pool, and a rinse-off under the rainforest shower in her suite, she placed a call to Irfan. The manager was there in minutes to escort her to breakfast before commencing an extensive tour of the grounds. He didn't volunteer Atu's whereabouts and she praised herself for not asking.

Still, she kicked herself when, a few minutes after she'd returned to the villa after a day spent exploring, her heart jumped when the phone on her bedside table rang.

'Hello. Did you miss me?'

His voice was a dark rasp that sent delicious unwanted shivers over her skin.

The sensation made her strike an offhand reply. 'Not at all. In fact, it's been a relief not to have you breathing down my neck.'

'And in amongst that relief did you enjoy yourself?'

She bit her lip. Answering *yes* would play into his hands. Answering *no* would be a lie. 'I need more than a day to make up my mind one way or another.'

'Of course you do. A word of caution, though. The careful approach doesn't win you any accolades.'

'What's that supposed to mean?'

'It means that every once in a while you need to be bold. Take what you want and to hell with everyone else.'

'Is that the way you operate?'

'Of course. Why else would I be so wildly successful?' he queried, with a devilish mockery which should have horrified her and yet aroused something in her that had gone dormant since his short absence.

The unnerving feeling escalated, making her shift in her chair. 'Was there a particular reason you called?'

He waited a beat, as if to let her pulse race faster for no other reason than waiting for him to speak. 'I called to let you know I'll be held up for another night.'

Amelie found herself biting her lip hard, with an unpleasant feeling dragging in her belly. Sternly reminding herself that what he did was none of her business didn't soothe her one iota.

'Amelie? Did you—?'

'I heard you. Like I said, you don't need to rush back on my account. Stay away as long as you like. Goodbye.'

She hung up before her voice got huskier. Before the sensation roiling in her stomach bled through into her voice.

There were three restaurants on the resort, one of them run by a Michelin-starred chef. There were numerous evening entertainments around the resort. She didn't have to stay in the villa on her own.

And yet she couldn't summon the interest to dress up and explore any of them.

Instead, she drummed up another weak jet-lag excuse, feeling a little guilty when Irfan commiserated and promised to send along her dinner.

Luckily, the feeling of unsettlement didn't follow her into sleep. She woke up rested and determined to put Atu out of her mind completely.

She donned her red-and-white-striped bikini, thought for a moment about taking a dip in her own pool, then decided a few laps in the bigger pool would set her up properly for the day ahead.

Her bare feet hardly made a sound as she walked through the villa, refusing even to glance towards Atu's as yet un-slept-in suite.

At the edge of the pool, she paused to dip her

toes in the water. The cool temperature was perfect, and she found herself smiling before catching herself. She wasn't supposed to enjoy herself like this. Was she?

Sure, at some point yesterday she'd accepted that if this partnership was with anyone else but a Quayson she would've been sorely tempted. But it was impossible. It would never work. Would it?

How would you know unless you try?

Her heart squeezed in recollection of her mother's accusation. But hadn't her late sister rebelled repeatedly and yet still been loved by her parents?

The mother she'd known as a child had been loving and considerate. A powerhouse socialite renowned for her hostess skills. Watching her mother effortlessly navigate charity galas and parties, expertly gliding through small talk, had shaped Amelie's own decision to become a hotelier. She'd dreamed of working alongside her sister and parents, expanding their small empire into something equalling the Quaysons'.

Losing her sister, then her father, had fractured that dream. But was it unthinkable that she and her mother could make it work if only her mother would come around?

She executed a perfect dive into the pool, hoping to silence the voice that urged her down a possibly rocky path.

Twenty minutes later she crawled lazily to the far side, resting her arms on the infinity edge and gazing at the waves leisurely lapping the shore thirty feet away.

When the tingling between her shoulder blades started, she assumed her muscles were simply reacting to the workout. But then that unique awareness arrived, making her belly clench for an entirely different reason.

She whipped her head around, the air locking in her lungs at the sight of Atu, standing on the edge of the pool, wearing a pair of navy swimming trunks that nearly made her swallow her tongue.

He was like a virile male god, moulded from the rich clay of their shared motherland. From the tips of his dense black closely cropped hair to the soles of his bare feet, he was…beautiful. Flawless in a way that made every cell in her body rush to painful life. It was as if he'd taken the oxygen with him when he left and was arrogantly gifting her the vital joy of breathing again now he was back.

For the life of her, Amelie couldn't find the

strength to be outraged. Because that emotion fizzing beneath her skin… It was pure delight.

'I… You're back,' she stated, then cringed at the breathy, inane statement.

Luckily, he didn't mock her for it. Instead, his gaze latched on her with vivid focus, making her aware of every bead of moisture clinging to her skin, the way her nipples pebbled beneath the water, the rush of heat between her thighs.

'I arrived late last night. You were already in bed.'

Was there a mild rebuke in there somewhere? She shook her head. Too many emotions were clashing against one another for her to decipher them properly.

'I was tired—and still a little jet-lagged,' she tagged on, in case he'd spoken to Irfan and knew of her excuse for staying indoors when she should have been socialising, making useful contacts for her resort.

He nodded, then turned to the lounge table a few feet away, drawing her attention to a wide, shallow tray piled high with breakfast delicacies. He picked it up and walked down the steps into the pool. When he was half submerged, he set the tray on the water and gently nudged it towards her.

Amelie barely glanced at the floating tray, her attention wholly absorbed in watching his smooth powerful strokes as he swam closer.

He arrived beside her, and his presence blocked out everything else but him.

'Do you feel better rested now?' he asked, and that low voice vibrated through her.

She swallowed. Her body's increasing tingling was mildly terrifying. 'Um…yes. Thanks.'

'I brought breakfast. Eat. You need your strength after that mammoth workout.'

Her gaze flitted to the glass walls of his bedroom. They were still opaque, not cleared by the remote control as she'd done hers, so she could enjoy her view of the rainforest. 'You were watching me?'

'It was difficult not to. You're a mesmerising swimmer.'

She shrugged, fighting off the treacherous thrill his compliment caused as he poured orange juice into two stout crystal glasses and held one out to her. She took a sip, welcoming the coolness, even though it did nothing to soothe her emotions.

Accepting a small plate of buttered toast from him, she ate a few mouthfuls. 'It was a matter of learning how to swim properly or be cowed into not learning at all.'

A frown appeared between his eyes. 'Who discouraged you?' he growled.

'No one in particular. But I was the youngest amongst our…the group, and sometimes my reluctance to get involved made your brothers and my male cousins impatient. I got my head dunked under the water a few too many times for my liking.'

Amelie noticed with mild surprise that the memory wasn't as bad as she'd imagined it would be. That, while the boys had been boisterous and even alarming back then, in hindsight it hadn't been so terrible. That a part of her wished she'd taken the time to enjoy those moments.

'So you took a bad situation and made it better?' he said, eyeing her with that unsettling intensity.

'There's no profound life lesson in there. I got fed up with swallowing chlorinated water and problem-solved by learning to be a strong swimmer. That's all.'

'I'm not sure what it says about me that I didn't notice.'

The words were murmured, almost as if he was questioning himself rather than her. But before she could read more into it, he slanted another glance at her.

'You never answered my question yesterday.'

She took her time to pour coffee, adding cream to hers and passing a black one to him. 'What question?'

He arched a brow at the coffee, and she realised she'd poured it the way he liked it. Her skin was just heating up with that bewildering faux pas when he replied, 'Did you miss me?'

The tight edge to the question should have irritated her. Instead, the fizzle beneath her skin intensified.

What the hell was wrong with her?

'I hardly think you need me to feed your male ego. Weren't your activities in Kuala Lumpur enough to scratch whatever itch you had?'

'Do I take it that waspish tone you took with me yesterday before hanging up was because you believe I was conducting more than just business in KL?'

'What you do and where you do it is none of my business, I'm sure.'

'Somehow I doubt that.'

'Excuse me?'

He took his time to pick up a tiny fork, spear a cube of melon and hold it to her lips. There was something almost decadent about being fed by him. Something she found irresistible.

Something she couldn't seem to keep fighting.

As she accepted and chewed the fruit, he replied, 'You're riled up…ready to cut me down with that beautiful tongue. Why? Because you believe I've been burning up another woman's sheets?'

'Have you?' she blurted out before she could stop herself. Then she held her breath, a large part of her terrified of his answer.

When had he drawn so close…so she needed to tilt her head to meet his gaze? How had she not noticed that his arms were now braced on either side of her waist in the pool, caging her in? That his gaze had grown all-consuming, sparking with a voracious hunger that echoed and pulsated low in her belly?

'As much as it disturbs me to admit it, I haven't been able to think about another woman besides you since you stormed back into my life.'

Her jaw sagged, and then her heart lurched, before banging so hard against her ribs she feared she would bruise. 'You… I…'

'It's almost gratifying to see you at a loss for words,' he said, lowering his head until they almost breathed the same air.

Every argument she'd had with herself thus far

unspooled in her head, growing weaker as it was dashed against the force of her desires.

She'd wanted this man since she was a teenager. Since he'd given her a painfully insufficient taste of him and she'd been introduced to true unquenchable hunger. And while she was admitting truths to herself, she begrudgingly accepted that the high bar he'd set in her fevered dreams all those years ago had set a standard the handful of men she'd dated since had fallen short of.

He was the reason her relationships had been lacklustre.

And, yes, she was breaking sacred rules by colluding with the enemy. But right in this moment, with heat blazing from his eyes, he didn't feel like the enemy. He felt like a euphoric drug she simply had to consume.

So take it! Take it now or you'll regret it...

Her heart quaked but she boldly met his gaze. 'Don't be so pleased about me being at a loss for words. In fact, you should pray for the opposite.'

A tremor moved through him. Then he stilled. 'Why?'

'Because then I can tell you what I want.'

The inferno built in his eyes, threatening to consume her. But his iron control held him rigid, even as his nostrils flared.

'Tell me,' he growled.

'I want you.' The words emerged in a hushed burst, laying her needs bare.

The arms braced on the pool tiles bunched hard, but still he held himself at bay, as if he didn't trust himself to draw any closer. From his haggard demeanour, he was hanging on by a thread.

'Be explicit, Amelie. Just so we're both clear,' he grated.

The wave of need and feminine power sweeping through her made her want to list every act she wanted him to perform on her. But in the end expediency won out. Because, dear God, she'd waited long enough.

Eight years.

'Take me to bed. Make love to me.'

The moment the words were out of her mouth he captured her waist and swung her out of the pool. With lithe, jaw-dropping strength, he vaulted out and swept her up into his arms, marching with single-minded purpose into the villa and down the wide hallway that led to the master suite.

Amelie couldn't tear her gaze away from the square jaw and stark hunger on his face. He was breathtaking.

Beautiful.

And when he kicked his bedroom door shut

and set her down beside his bed, with his fingers trailing down to link with her own for a few moments, she felt beautiful too. Truly wanted for the first time in a very long while.

Here, now, with his gaze raking over her face with such blatant need that an exhilarating thrill coursed through her body, she wasn't an afterthought or a reliable combatant to hold the line against an enemy.

She was Amelie Hayford—a woman with long-buried needs about to be fulfilled.

He reached behind her and slowly untied the strings of her bikini top, letting it drop without a care where it landed.

With ease that testified to his strength, he plucked her up again and placed her in the middle of the bed. Then he stood back.

Eyes squarely pinned on her, he trailed a finger over her cheek, along her jaw, then down her neck. She trembled when he lingered on the pulse beating there, then continued the sizzling path down between her breasts.

Her nipples furled into tight points, and it felt all the more maddening when he ignored them and caressed his way further south to her belly button before reversing direction.

This time when he reached her breasts he

palmed one mound, then swallowed hard as she moaned.

'God. You're beautiful.'

'Atu…'

Lean, strong fingers hooked into her bikini bottoms, yanking them off in one smooth move.

Completely naked, Amelie felt like a decadent offering, lying there under the heat of his gaze. Heart slamming hard against her ribs, she started to reach for him, but he caught and pinned her arms above her head, leaning down to take her mouth in a consuming kiss.

Her moan was uninhibited. The thrill of his hands on her body was sending her straight into that sublime place where pleasure lingered, beckoning her into deeper bliss.

Her cry of protest when he pulled away a minute later made him smile. His gaze travelled over her, as if he was committing the curves and valleys of her body to memory.

Planting a knee on the bed, he lowered his face back to hers and took her mouth in another deep kiss. This time he didn't restrain her, and Amelie curled one hand over his nape, holding him to her as she parted her lips for him, savoured him hungrily.

Again, he ended the kiss far too soon, his

tongue travelling down her neck, licking over her pulse before going lower.

She gasped as his hand palmed her breast again, toying with her nipple until her back arched off the bed. Until fevered sensation rippled like a restless tide over her.

And when his mouth dropped to capture one peak in his mouth, Amelie gave a tortured moan. Her fingers bit into his shoulder and she revelled in the answering shudder through his body. He tormented her for several minutes, then journeyed south, peppering kisses over her flesh.

'Let me see you,' he demanded gutturally. 'Show me what I crave.'

She gave a helpless moan as her thighs fell wide open. For a charged spell, he simply stared down at her core, his eyes burning flames of need. Then he passed the pads of his fingers over her damp flesh.

Pleasure rippled through, intensified when he seemed absorbed with watching her every reaction to his touch. 'So soft… So responsive…'

'Please…'

His nostrils flared as he shamelessly basked in his masculine prowess and the knowledge that she was putty in his hands.

The need to reciprocate, to tug him under her

mercy as he was doing to her, made her surge upright. His eyes flashed at her, but she ignored the imperious command she was sure hovered on his lips and grasped him through his trunks.

He hissed, his body jerking against her hold. 'Amelie…' he warned hoarsely.

'Do you want me to stop?' she asked, more than a little awed by the power and thickness of him.

A muscle ticked in his jaw for a second or two. Then he firmly removed her hand from his rigid shaft. 'You'll get your chance later.'

With that, he pushed her firmly back onto the bed and dragged her thighs wider apart.

Casting one last searing look at her face, he lowered his head to her. His carnal kiss was bold, arrogant and sublime. There was no hesitancy in his sampling of her. His tongue owned her in broad strokes that had her head rolling back on the pillow.

'Oh…oh, God!'

Firm hands held her still as she trembled, sensation piling high with every lick, every kiss. She curled her fingers into his thick hair, torn between pushing him away so she wasn't wholly consumed by this insane fever and holding him closer to speed up the rush of ecstasy.

But Atu danced to his own tune, dragging her

right to the brink, then retreating until she was sure she would go out of her mind.

Fierce brown eyes rose to lock with hers, eagerly absorbing every gasp, every breathless plea, while his tongue continued to wreck her.

'Oh, God…please!'

Redirecting his lips to that bundle of nerves, he thrust two fingers inside her.

Amelie's groan of pleasure bounced off the walls as she careened once more to the edge of bliss. But he'd driven her there countless times, and she was suddenly terrified he would leave her there. Her abdomen clenched and she held her breath, her gaze still locked with his.

'So strong. So stubborn. Give it up,' he growled hotly. 'Come for me.'

Her scream of release drowned out his grunt of satisfaction as she let go, her body contorting with searing bliss that ravaged every nerve ending, altering her from the inside out.

She felt his lips leave her core, trail up her body as she continued to shiver and burn. He dropped a branding kiss on her mouth before she felt him move away.

Through lust-drenched eyes she watched him shuck off his trunks. Then she shivered once more at the sight of his impressive shaft.

He reached into the bedside drawer and withdrew a foil packet. Donning the protection, he prowled back onto the bed.

'Do you know how long I've thought about this?' he rasped against her lips.

She squeezed her eyes shut, desperate to savour every moment. 'No, I don't.'

He gave a low, almost self-deprecating laugh. 'Yes, you do. We've both wanted this for far too long.'

He arranged her so that her back was flush against his heated front, then hooked an arm beneath one thigh. With his other hand, he caressed her nape in a sensual hold. Then, with his eyes on hers, Atu thrust hard inside her, burying himself to the hilt.

Amelie cried out at the tumult of sensation, at the fullness of him, the power and potency of his possession making her eyes roll. His answering groan as he withdrew and penetrated her once more started a chain reaction inside her she couldn't have held back if she'd tried.

She didn't even attempt it.

For so long she'd craved this. Now it was hers. *He* was hers…for now.

She reached back and curled her hand over his nape, holding on for dear life as sensation built and built, then tossed her over the edge into sheer bliss.

Atu held her, his fingers digging into her hip, as she shuddered through her climax. Then, just as she was catching her breath, he flipped her over, dragged her hips up until she was on all fours, then stroked back inside her.

Amelie suspected that he was branding her in a way that would remain with her for ever.

She clutched the sheets and held on for dear life as he sent her soaring once more. Words, time and space ceased to have meaning. Her body was a mere instrument which he used to show her how he could master her every sense.

And when her next release claimed her, he permitted her only a short respite before he flipped her over again, his sweat-slicked body bracing against hers as he kissed her long and deep, then drew back.

'Again, Amelie,' he ordered hoarsely.

And, sweet heaven help her, she was helpless to resist.

He'd stayed away as long as he could. At first he'd been righteously adamant that business justified his being away. But when the meetings were over and he still stayed away, Atu knew he was actively avoiding Amelie. Avoiding rekindling that moment of almost *intimate* common ground he'd felt discussing their shared experiences with their parents. The feeling that she *understood* him. Perhaps wouldn't judge him for the choices he'd made.

But the longer he'd stayed away, the more resentful he'd been for allowing *emotion* to keep him away. Especially when he'd promised himself emotion would never be the basis of his actions.

Finding himself outside her door late last night after a mad dash flight from Kuala Lumpur that his pilot was probably still disgruntled about, his urge to knock, to see her, had confirmed that something had shifted irreparably.

He couldn't stop thinking about Amelie Hayford. She was wedged firmly under his skin. And not even the phone calls he was avoiding from his brother and father—calls he knew he'd have to answer soon—were enough to dissuade him from taking what he wanted.

Taking her...

Last night he'd forced himself to retreat to his own room and buried himself in even more work until sleep had claimed him.

The sound of her diving into the pool this morning had roused him from sleep. He'd stood at his window, hypnotised by her smooth glide through the water. A nugget of a memory had sharpened, and he'd recalled that she'd been part of her swim team at her boarding school, winning more than a few awards.

He'd shaken his head when he'd realised he hadn't moved in twenty minutes. Something about this woman commanded his attention to the exclusion of all else.

With another bracing twist of memory, he'd accepted that perhaps he needed to cut his late brother some slack—because if this was even a sliver of what Fiifi had felt for the other Hayford sister...

He'd clenched his jaw.

No, he'd told himself. He was confusing lust with the overblown emotions triggered by his brother's melodramatic relationship with the older Hayford sister.

And when he'd changed into his swimming gear and ordered breakfast for them both, he'd told himself it was simply to progress the reason they were at this resort in the first place.

Now, as he thrust inside her, with the most sublime sensations buffeting him, even as a stark hunger clawed through him, making him wonder if he'd ever get enough of her, he knew that every reason except *this* had been a secondary pretext.

The feel of her…vibrant, passionate…her sultry voice moaning his name as bliss swept her away… It smashed the ennui he'd been living in to smithereens. But what was more disturbing— what he needed to get a handle on as quickly as possible—was this out-of-control feeling.

And what better way than by doing this? Drowning himself in her tight, supple body?

With a roar that seemed dragged from his very soul, he claimed his release, and felt another wave of bewilderment sweeping over him at the depth of his need. At the faint voice that whispered its doubt that his need of her might ever wane.

It will, he stressed to himself as he collapsed next to her, their bodies slick and their breath panting. As he pulled her close and revelled in the sexual aftershocks that shivered through her body. *It had to.*

Because he wanted her resort—perhaps now more than ever. For one thing, he abhorred the idea of Amelie falling into the clutches of some greedy corporate shark—and, yes, he intended to ignore *that* irony. And also, while he knew he'd meet resistance from his father, Amelie's passion about her resort would come in handy when he took over.

Is that all?

He ignored the taunting query and pulled her closer, unable to resist caressing her firm flesh. Then he tensed as her brown eyes darkened with a touch of wariness.

'What is it?' he asked.

She slicked her tongue over plump lips swollen from his kisses. 'This has happened so quickly...'

'On the contrary. I believe this was long over-due.'

She bit the corner of her lip, her wariness intensifying. 'I know we agreed to sex for the sake of...of getting a handle on this thing between us...'

He didn't feel the need to state that, while theirs was a chemistry unlike any other, he was disillusioned enough to know that despite what he'd felt a few minutes ago this too would pass. In a month from now, perhaps even in less time, he would be back in that jaded place, ennui once again his companion.

But for now he intended to enjoy the thrill of the chase.

Are you sure that's all it is?

He brushed away the irritating question that

whispered at the back of his mind, scoffing at what else it might be.

She worried her lip again and his stomach tightened further.

'If you're about to pump the brakes, it's too late. That particular horse has bolted, Amelie.'

Her eyes sparked, and he wanted to smile through the unsettled sensations spiking through him. *Awuraze*, her spirit was intoxicating. One thing he was certain of was that, whatever time they had together, boredom wouldn't be their problem.

'I wasn't going to… I don't regret it,' she murmured.

Atu despised the magnitude of his relief, which threatened to evaporate almost immediately. 'But…?'

'But…for however long this lasts… I don't want anyone to know.'

It took a few moments for him to grasp her meaning. Then rebellion clenched hard in his gut. 'What?'

Her sweet chin lifted, her beautiful features gaining a resolute look that further hardened his insides. 'You heard me. I want strict discretion.'

He pushed back from her, a ragged disgruntlement building inside him as he realised she meant every word.

'I'm not some sleazy secret to be kept under wraps,' he growled.

He was Atu Quayson.

Powerful. Influential.

He'd been born with the proverbial silver spoon in his mouth, but he'd carved his own stratospheric path, thereby gaining choices few men were privileged to have. With a simple phone call he could have a dozen women ready to jump to do his bidding. Not the other way around.

But, perversely, knowing he had the power to grant her wish made him withhold it. Shedding his control now would only make him weak.

'I detest secrets,' he bit out, memories of keeping Fiifi's intention to walk away from his family and the tragedy that had led to churning through him. Perhaps if he'd forced his brother to state his intentions openly, and if he hadn't been so wrapped up in his own dejection, Fiifi would still be alive. 'Especially unnecessary ones. If you're with me, we own our affair.'

The flash of understanding in her eyes came and went far too quickly, but he felt it to his core. Just as he felt the flicker of misgiving that replaced it.

He tilted her face to his, registering her smooth, supple skin. 'Tell me you want me,' he commanded, a need to hear her confirmation swelling inside him.

She licked her lower lip, making him stifle a groan as he waited impatiently.

'I want you,' she confirmed huskily.

'Then have me. Without reservations.'

'Wouldn't that make me a blind fool?'

'It would make you a woman who sees what she wants and takes it.' His hand slid down her neck to the pulse racing at her throat, then lower, over one breast to her pounding heart. 'The woman underneath this, who is straining to loosen the reins of obligation holding her back.'

She made a small keening sound filled with need and he couldn't help himself. He pressed his advantage. Because that was the sort of man he was. Wasn't that one of the many accusations his father had levelled at him? As if the same single-mindedness his parent now demanded he use to cement the Quayson legacy was a flaw.

He moulded her breast, flicking his thumb over her erect nipple. She gasped against his lips and, devil take him, he needed her to come apart. Needed to make her feel the same fever that hadn't abated one iota from his blood.

Rising from the bed, he disposed of the condom, then swept her up once more. A few steps and they were at his plunge pool. He walked them through the warm water, then deposited her on the wide divan bed set on the pedestal in the middle of the pool.

Dappled sunlight bathed them as her fevered eyes met his, her lips slightly parted as she panted softly. 'Atu… What…?'

'I haven't come anywhere close to having my fill of you. Don't deny me.'

Hearing the hint of a plea in his own words further perplexed him. Where the hell was his famed control?

For a suspended heartbeat, she held her breath. Then it whooshed out softly as she shook her head. And when he positioned himself lower on the bed, her eyes widened into shocked orbs.

'Again?'

He laughed under his breath. 'Oh, yes, sweet Amelie,' he rasped, firmly pushing her back until she was propped up on her elbows as he boldly parted her thighs.

Atu couldn't take his eyes off her. She glowed under the Malaysian sun, with fat drops of water he wanted to lick off clinging to her smooth skin.

But her intoxicating scent was calling to him, and he was helpless to resist.

His breath threatened to strangle him as he trailed kisses over her inner thighs and over the perfectly groomed trail of curls framing her feminine core. With a low, hungry growl, he slicked his tongue over her.

Her sweet cry was music to his ears. Yes, he wanted her as driven and helpless as he felt—wanted her to be mindless with only thoughts of him.

So he parted her wider, savoured and feasted until her head rolled back on her shoulders. Until her breaths panted from her and his name punctuated her husky moans.

Only then did he centre his attention on her clitoris, swirling his tongue expertly over the swollen bundle of nerves until she cried out sharply.

Atu held her until her breathing quieted. When he tugged her into his arms, he sensed her confusion.

'Don't you…? Aren't you…?'

Her gaze darted from his in a surprisingly coy way that gave a hint of her relative innocence. And why the hell did *that* reignite a primitive blaze inside him?

Before temptation overtook him, he rose from

the bed. He'd wanted to remind her of how combustible they were together, and he'd done that. Now he needed to wrestle back some control before his foundations were breached irreparably.

'I need to return a few calls before the business day ends in Ghana.'

The blatant desire in her eyes as her gaze drifted over him threw a thin balm over the sensations roiling inside him. But as he walked away, he suspected that little victory might mean nothing unless he succeeded in keeping his fast-dwindling control...

Amelie watched Atu walk away with her heart lodged firmly in her throat. She wasn't sure which stunned her more—the sublime sex Atu had just gifted her or the fact that it had left her needing him more... Even now, as her body throbbed in the aftermath, her senses still awash with her release, she craved him again.

She dragged the sheet over her chest, pleased he hadn't stuck around to witness how totally swept away she'd been by the act, how completely she'd immersed herself in the experience of being possessed by him. The man she'd secretly crushed on since her teenage years.

That dismaying feeling was why she'd blurted

out the need for discretion. It had stemmed entirely from the compelling need to do the opposite. To throw caution to the wind and claim him, if only temporarily.

To desire, regardless of the consequences, the way her sister had.

As she sank back onto the bed, another thought struck her. Atu had only asked how she was enjoying his resort since his return. He hadn't applied the intense pressure she'd expected. It was almost as if he was content to step back and let the magic of Q Cove work itself into her consciousness.

Was she wrong about him? Or was it a calculated exercise in patience meant to lower her defences?

Her mind drifted back to what had happened minutes ago. He'd gifted her sublime pleasure and, despite his blatant need, he'd walked away.

Against her will, something softened inside her, which then opened the door to possibilities she'd convinced herself were forbidden to her.

An association with a Quayson.

Perhaps even a chance that this thing between them didn't have to end so soon.

Her heart shuddered as she rose from the bed, quickly washed off in the pool, and then, wrapped in a bathrobe, returned to her suite.

Was it even possible? Or was she letting herself be swayed by his words…letting the freedom of being away from responsibility prompt her into dreams that had no hope of becoming reality?

Dressed in capri trousers and a flowery top, she emerged half an hour later to find Atu in the living room, looking out at the pool. Suddenly self-conscious, Amelie averted her gaze. She would probably never look at another swimming pool without recalling the intensely sexual moments she'd experienced today.

But it wasn't as easy to avert her gaze from *him*.

As if sensing her scrutiny, his head whipped towards her, his gaze charting her body the way she'd done with his. 'Good, you're dressed.'

She nodded. 'Where are we going?'

His lips twitched. 'No need to look so wary, Amelie. It will be enjoyable.'

She pressed her lips together, fighting the urge to blurt out the confusing questions she was grappling with. To seek some sort of assurance that all this wouldn't end up in more heartache for her.

But how could she without sounding the opposite of the strong, capable woman she'd insisted she was? Hadn't Atu himself declared how disillusioned he was with women who displayed over-blown emotions? Seeking emotional assurances from him a mere hour after they'd made love was as good as inviting him to pigeonhole her.

His eyes narrowed, tension zipping the space between them. 'Amelie?'

She suppressed the ripples of agitation and smiled. 'I'm ready.'

For a long moment he stared at her, then nodded. 'Let's go, then.'

A gleaming top-of-the-range four-by-four waited for them at Reception. They drove into the rainforest, where he produced two pairs of binoculars and introduced her to the thrills of wildlife spotting. Dusky leaf monkeys, oriental pied hornbills and even a rare eagle dazzled her senses. Time passed in a colourful blur of heady experiences, and before she knew it, they stood beneath the canopy of soaring trees.

Amelie glanced nervously at the long ropes dangling from them and the geared-up attendants nearby. 'I know I picked abseiling as one of the activities, but it may have been a mistake.'

A sober look settled over his face. 'Maybe it was. But are you going to pass up the chance to view reality from a different perspective?'

Something clenched inside her. He wasn't referring to just abseiling. But suddenly, when she would have challenged him before, trepidation held her back. Because the gathering certainty that she *did* want to look at life from a different lens wouldn't leave her.

It was a relief to throw herself into the exhilarating but mildly terrifying abseil from the top of the meranti trees, leaving her muddled thoughts far below. But when they reached the bottom, and Atu put his arm around her waist and drew her close, every apprehensive sensation came rushing back.

They still lingered as she dressed for dinner several hours later.

Her rich purple and green *dashiki* dress moulded her body from chest to hip, before lightly flaring to her ankles, and the spaghetti straps ensured she kept cool in the humid temperature. She'd rolled up a matching scarf into a headdress, before securing jade-green chandelier earrings.

A spritz of her favourite perfume, a quick glide of dark plum lip gloss before stepping into thin-strapped heels, and she was done.

Atu was stepping out of his own suite as she left hers.

He froze at the sight of her, his fierce scrutiny making her aware of every inch of exposed flesh.

'Ahwofe dua,' he announced huskily. 'You look intoxicating.'

Ahwofe dua—loosely translated as beauty tree. She felt her face heat in a blush. Then her whole body followed suit as he smiled and every cell in her body reacted to the drop-dead effect of his handsomeness.

'Thank you,' she murmured around a suddenly clogged throat.

His heated gaze stayed on her for a few more beats. 'Come,' he instructed, holding out his arm to her. 'Our culinary adventure awaits.'

They took a buggy, leisurely winding through paved stone paths bordered with miniature palms and wide-leafed plants that she brushed her fingers through as they passed. The air was perfumed with the scent of exotic flowers, reminding her of her own lovingly tended shrubbery back at her own resort.

They pulled up at the base of a large acacia tree, and Amelie's jaw dropped as she lifted her gaze.

The restaurant was laid out across three large trees, intricately linked with platforms and walkways and illuminated with miniature lanterns strung together and woven through the trees.

He led her up a spiral staircase built into the trunk of the tree. Across the wooden gangway, their table was set on the middle platform, pristine flatware gleaming on a white tablecloth and a view of the setting sun on the ocean creating yet another magnificent scene.

Once the waiter had uncorked and poured vintage white wine, and the master chef had personally delivered their freshly prepared tempura and sushi, Atu eyed her over the rim of his glass.

'Are you going to finally admit that you like my resort?'

She bit her lip, then nodded. 'Yes. It's beautiful.'

The expected smugness didn't arrive. Instead, he nodded solemnly, his gaze lingering over his creation.

'Why Malaysia?' she prodded, after they'd eaten a few bites.

A touch of cynicism twisted his lips, but his gaze stayed on the beach a moment longer before he replied. 'It was nothing profound. I packed a bag, boarded my jet and instructed my pilot to take me wherever he chose. He's half-Malaysian. He brought me to his home. I hired a jeep, drove all over for a month and ended up here. The possibility of what this place could be took hold. Delivered the purpose I needed.'

She swallowed the question that attempted to spill free, but it rose again in the next breath. 'What made you pack a bag? Why did you leave Ghana?'

The clenched fingers on his glass and the downward sweep of his gaze said he wasn't in the mood to answer. But she curbed the urge to switch to safer subjects. She'd shared her body with this man. Perhaps she was foolish to allow a sliver of emotion to sneak into every intoxicating sensation he evoked in her, but she couldn't halt the need sweeping through her. The urge to delve beneath his surface.

After an age staring into the light golden contents of his glass, he raised his head. 'I found that I didn't want to step into the still-warm shoes of my recently deceased brother.'

She winced, her heart squeezing for him, her own fingers tightening around her wine glass.

'Not after being assured over and over again that I was second-best,' he added.

Had things really been that bad?

'It wasn't a secret that you butted heads with your father from time to time, but he was always boasting about your accomplishments. You and Ekow's—not just Fiifi's.'

A chilled look swept over his face. 'He was very skilled in projecting the exact image he wanted. It didn't suit him to announce that he favoured one son over the others. My mother, of course, went along with whatever he decreed.

Including insisting that I assume every role that had been laid out for the heir apparent after they lost their precious son.'

'You're not their firstborn, but was taking on the mantle so bad?' she dared, then watched his eyes freeze over completely.

'You mean like you did?' he queried in a cool voice. A voice unlike that of the lover who'd lavished her with sublime passion this morning.

Despite his coolness, she didn't shy away from answering. Because it was what she'd done. And, despite her mother's censure, she believed she'd done a good job. 'Yes.'

But it wasn't enough. It might never be...

She suppressed a dart of desolation as he answered.

'Yes. It turned out I wasn't very adept at playing the diplomat, you see. I had strong opinions, which I expressed freely and frequently.'

Amelie took a bolstering gulp of wine, memory flitting through her brain. 'Fiifi was strong-willed too, but he was also the type to—'

'Pretend to bend to accommodate his heritage and destiny. It was his talent. While I was deemed rigid. *Unaccommodating.*'

She peered closer at him, the urge to know him digging deeper, despite the beginnings of tension arrowing across the table at her. 'Pretend? What does that mean?'

'It means he was better at playing the heir than I could ever have been. Until he decided to abandon the game altogether.'

Despite the chilling bitterness in his voice, she felt his pain. Wanted to wrap her arms around him. She resisted.

'I can't tell whether you liked him or loathed him for not being alive.'

An almost haunted look wove through the chill. 'He allowed himself to be led astray by lofty ideas and emotions. Saying I would give anything to have him back won't change anything, but I regret not acting sooner to convince him that his so-called love was nothing but wishful thinking. I regret not having the chance to talk him out of it.'

Goosebumps prickled her arms, a chill sweeping over her at his words. 'You wanted the chance to talk him out of...falling in love?'

'You sound horrified,' he observed with stony accuracy. 'Why? It's the truth. You opened this can of worms, Amelie. I believe it's on you if you don't like its contents.'

CHAPTER EIGHT

AMELIE WASN'T SURE how the atmosphere had shifted so suddenly. But now the subject had exploded between them, there was no going back.

'What you said to me on the plane… Do you think Fiifi moulded himself into what my sister wanted? Is that why you said their relationship was a lie?'

He stiffened. Then the thunderous look in his eyes turned into resentment. 'It's my turn to regret this subject being brought up.'

'Why? I thought I was the one who was too timid to confront reality.'

His lips twisted, but no sign of humour lightened his face. 'Touché.'

She pressed her lips together and waited. And waited. 'So…?'

'I didn't say their relationship was a lie. But they believed themselves to be in love. And love is a lie.'

His utter conviction reached across the table and wrapped its merciless talons around her chest, crushing her with each breath. 'What?'

Eyes bleak with the certainty of his belief met hers. 'They had a chemical reaction to each other, which they falsely believed to be a grand cosmic event they were prepared to risk everything for. And to what end?'

'Because it was worth nurturing? Worth building a life on?'

'What life? One where they eventually tired of each other and realised they were trapped? Or one where they brought children into the world only to play favourites because there wasn't enough *love* to go around?'

She set her glass down before she spilled her wine. 'You really think all relationships have a short shelf life?'

He shrugged. 'I've yet to be proved wrong so far.'

'What about your parents?'

His face tightened. 'Obligation. Duty. I don't have a problem with agreed unions that have mutually beneficial goals, provided both parties enter into it with their eyes wide open. What I have a problem with is basing a relationship on false promises and failing to nurture the children you bring into the world.'

With each pronouncement, she felt something wither inside her. 'How long have you felt like this?'

'What does it matter?'

She gave up any pretence of finishing her meal, her appetite gone. 'I simply want to know if this cynicism is reversible or whether you're a lost cause.'

The formidable and ruthless Atu Quayson was roused into life then, his narrow-eyed gaze piercing her where she sat. 'I'd advise you against any virtuous notions of changing my mind. You won't succeed.'

Somehow she managed to summon a small, self-assured smile, even as her insides churned. 'Are you sure? You've labelled me stubborn on countless occasions, if I recall.'

For a moment he seemed almost perturbed. Then his lips flattened. 'You're not the first to try. What makes you think you'll succeed where others have failed?'

The notion that other women had tried to change him sent acid flooding through her system. She pushed the sensation away, refusing to accommodate it when she was fighting for something that felt...vital.

'Because I'm me. The woman you want—perhaps only in this moment, according to you. But I'm also a Hayford. We have a connection. Perhaps a similar connection to the one your brother had with my sister. You have confessed that I drive you insane, after all.'

He shifted in his seat, as if her words had stirred his frozen soul. 'But, unlike her, you will not die. I forbid it.'

The utterly cavalier way in which he decreed it drew a bark of laughter from her. 'You do, do you?'

'Yes. I would prefer you stick around for a while.'

'Why?'

His eyes positively smouldered, branding and possessing her from across the table. 'Because now I've had you, I regret not doing so long before now. I don't intend to let you go until I've had my fill of you. And you're not allowed to take yourself out of my immediate sphere until I do.'

Electricity and need, affront and that roller-coaster sensation all became live wires within her, snaking and twisting and snapping until she didn't know whether she wanted to jump up and run away, or reach across the table and drag his arrogant head to her and kiss the living daylights out of him.

The effort it took to contain it had her bunching her fists in her lap, the remains of her meal forgotten as she stared at him. 'This…this is why you're called the black sheep, isn't it? You're not a rebel or a playboy or even a disruptor. You're simply utterly ruthless in what you want and to hell with everyone else. And your father didn't like that about you, did he? At least, not at first? He wanted you to be a team player. On a team he fully controlled. And you refused, didn't you?'

A grim smile snagged the corners of his lips for a nanosecond. 'Yes, I did. He lost his first-born and decided his second would be the perfect replica. Only he didn't ask my permission, nor care that I wanted to be my own person. I didn't change for him. I don't intend to change for anyone else.'

He knocked back the last of his drink and set the glass firmly on the table. He was back to his true diabolical self.

But for a single moment in time she wondered if it was all true. Whether there wasn't a part of him…the part she'd caught a glimpse of in bed this morning…that wasn't layering on this mantle of brutishness to protect himself from the indifference shown him by his father?

One eyebrow slowly lifted, as if daring her to voice that tiny misgiving.

When someone shows you who they are, believe them the first time.

That memorable quote whispered through her head.

'Tell me something, Atu. When all of this is done…when this chemistry wears itself out…will you go away and never think of me again?'

Again, he started, fisting his hands on the table before he consciously relaxed them. 'When all of this is done, unless you change your mind about selling outright to me, you'll retain a vested interest in your resort. That means our paths will likely cross from time to time.'

She wanted to reply that she didn't mean professionally. But she already felt so raw and vulnerable. The parts of her that continued to wish for *personal*, not business, for *affection* instead of blueprints, were leaving her more and more exposed.

A waiter approached and asked if they would like dessert. With her vanished appetite showing no signs of returning, Amelie shook her head.

Atu rose and helped her out of her chair. Casting her another piercing look, he held out his arm.

Still caught in this curious dance they seemed to be doing, she stood and slipped her hand into the crook of his elbow.

Their trip back to the villa was conducted in silence.

Her heels clicked as she walked into the hall. Then her feet seemed to slow of their own accord. She heard him come up behind her, pause a foot away. Heard him inhale long and deep. Then his hands were cupping her shoulders.

'Join me for a nightcap?' It was part request, mostly command.

Logic prompted her to say no, but she found herself nodding instead. He rubbed his hands up and down her bare arms once, then moved away.

She followed him into the living room, watching as he crossed over to the extensive liquor cabinet before her attention was drawn to the window.

Outside, the rainforest was settling for the night, trees swaying gently and the muted sounds of animals calling to each other providing soft background music.

She accepted the mystery drink he handed her. She tasted it, her eyes widening in surprise at the rich tartness and fizz that exploded on her tongue.

'Good?'

'Very. Thank you.'

He inclined his head, then crossed over to settle on the sofa. 'I met with my architects while I was in KL.'

'If you're going to push me about the resort—'

'I don't need to. Irfan has kept me informed about your in-depth tour of the place. You wouldn't be so interested if you weren't already invested. I also know you'll work your way through to saying yes to me when you're ready. But the new blueprints for your resort are almost completed.'

She tensed, several darts of hurt spiking through her. 'If you've already started the process without me, why are you bothering to tell me?'

His shoulder twitched in a shrug. There was not one iota of remorse for his actions on his face. 'I saw no point in wasting time.'

'I haven't said yes.'

Yet.

The word hovered between them. With every passing second, she was more convinced this was the only right way forward.

'We're not leaving just yet. Whatever changes you wish to make to the blueprints can be made. In the meantime, feel free to take your time about capitulating to me. I'll do my best to hold back my impatience.'

Her breath caught. 'Can you actually breathe

up on that mountain of arrogance where you insist on dwelling?'

He sat back…no, *sprawled* back in his seat, his arms spreading out to rest on the top of the sofa, a fatuous smile on his face. She wanted to wipe it off.

'The air is perfectly fine up here. And so is the view. You should join me.'

A part of her hated that he was right.

Everything she'd discovered about Q Cove had made her fall in love with the place. She knew now why it was booked solid months in advance.

Another part of her hated that his complete and utter self-assurance was so sexy. So…*arousing.*

'I'm perfectly fine where I am, thank you,' she said, cringing when her voice emerged a tad too primly.

'Are you?' he invited, his body still relaxed, on display, effortlessly disrupting her breathing and her ability to form coherent thoughts. 'Then why do you stare at me with longing in your eyes?'

She gasped. 'I wasn't—'

With an impatient growl, he leaned forward and pressed his thumb to her lips, silencing her. Her heart leapt in her chest, and her outrage was nowhere to be found as he proceeded to explore the outline of her lips in a heated, leisurely fashion.

'There's nothing wrong with wanting, Amelie.'

She felt herself sway forward, then quickly caught herself. 'Good. Then you won't mind that I've taken Irfan's advice and booked Assan for tomorrow morning. So whatever plans you have will have to wait until I've experienced his sublime massage that everyone's recommending.'

He stiffened and his eyes flashed, right before he withdrew his touch.

She immediately wished it back.

'Is that so?'

'You don't sound very pleased about that...' She was poking a sleeping tiger. And yet she couldn't stop.

He shrugged, but she suspected he wasn't as carefree as he pretended.

Abruptly, his hand returned to her face, whispering a caress down her cheek. 'If that is what you wish for, then that's what you'll have.'

Her breath shuddered out of her when his caress continued down her neck to the juncture of her shoulder, down her arm to circle her wrist.

Slowly, keeping his eyes on hers, he lifted it to his mouth. The kiss he deposited on the inside of her wrist was slow, exploratory, as her pulse beat against his lips.

'If you're done with your nightcap, I'd very

much like to pick up where I left off this morning,' he said thickly.

And because she now knew what making love with Atu entailed, knew that the purest strain of pleasure awaited her, she let herself melt into his arms, quietly reassuring herself that now she knew his true stance on entanglements she was well-armed against hurt.

Atu felt her ripple around him in her third release and knew he was about to be driven clean out of his mind. Yet he couldn't get enough of her.

Perhaps that should have been his first inkling that this thing with Amelie was different from any other liaison. Even while he was inside her he already dreaded when it would be over.

A novelty in itself, he mused darkly to himself several hours later, that he was suffering from separation anxiety, when he was usually the first to leave a woman's bed.

Beside him, the woman he'd taken repeatedly throughout the night slept soundly, one hand curled on his chest. Her sweet cries had filled his ears and topped up his satisfaction. Now daylight filtered through the trees of the rainforest, and he was caught in the rare position of being…
unsettled.

Perhaps it had something to do with that question she'd asked him at dinner last night.

'When all of this is done, will you go away and never think of me again?'

She shifted beside him and he looked down into her beautiful face. Her lips were slightly parted, her breathing steady.

Would he miss her?

Why did he need to contemplate that question now? They had time. At the very least, time to indulge in more of this. And time to complete the project he was almost certain she would come on board with.

So why delve deeper into the emotions he'd sworn never to explore now?

He shifted, still a little dismayed that he'd let his guard down so spectacularly last night. Broached questions he should've left alone, reopening old wounds that should have healed by now but still festered just below the surface.

Perhaps he'd been raw from the phone call with his father when he'd left Amelie in bed that morning.

The old man's health might be failing at an alarming rate, with the heart disease he'd ignored for far too long putting him out of reach of effective medical intervention, but his bark still packed a punch.

While he knew that there was no way he could manipulate his second son into doing his bidding, his father still found a way to make his voice heard—as he had done repeatedly during their phone call.

His father's displeasure as to why progress had not yet been made on the Saltpond project had been evident. Atu's response that things would get done at his own pace had triggered the usual torrent of disagreement.

And, as usual, his mother had stepped in to make the peace, pretending not to take sides, but inevitably falling in with her husband's wishes.

He'd been more than relieved to end the call. Even more thankful that he was halfway around the world. Why had he delved back into the subject of his dysfunctional relationships when Amelie had asked last night? Especially when he rarely spoke of his relationship with his father?

Hell, he hadn't just answered her questions— he'd volunteered a torrent of personal, private details.

What the hell was wrong with him?

The question pinged around in his brain with no resolution. And when the answer was taken out of his hands by the movement of her body against his, he eagerly allowed the distraction.

His body roared into life, eager to explore this new and mind-melting avenue so he wouldn't have to think about his family with its tragic flaws and bitterness and indifference. An avenue where the only thing that existed was the surprisingly passionate generosity of a unique woman.

She opened her eyes and for a moment he saw sweet confusion flit over her face. Primitive pleasure fizzed through him at the coyness that washed over her face, and then a sweet smile curved her sensual lips.

'I could hear you thinking in my sleep. I wish you hadn't done it so loudly.'

He felt his lips curve in a smile, and for the first time he didn't mind the morning-after awkwardness that lingered only briefly before he put a stop to it all by bending down and taking her lips in a kiss that started off lightly but gathered strength, unravelling him as it heated up.

Half an hour later his senses were still reeling, and the state of confusion he was getting mired in had only worsened.

He glanced towards the bedroom she'd disappeared into after their shower together, fighting the urge to go to her when he was finished dressing.

Whatever this unsettling feeling was, it would dissipate with time.

They had history. A charged history that had always meant this association wouldn't be as smooth as all his others. Nothing more.

And as for that voice that mocked him for his reluctance to dig deeper? He ignored it.

CHAPTER NINE

AMELIE'S HAND TIGHTENED on the phone, her mother's sorrow and fury rolling over her in waves that made her stomach clench in despair.

Perhaps she should have waited until her roller-coaster emotions had quieted. But they'd shown no signs of doing so after ten days spent in Atu's bed.

Sweet heaven, the feelings he'd dragged from her... Elation. Wonder. Yearning. Passion she wouldn't have believed she was capable of before that first night.

So what if threaded through those feelings was a quiet despair that Atu Quayson didn't believe in love? Hadn't she concurred with him that theirs was only a strong chemistry which would dissipate once they'd explored it? What did love have to do with it?

She shied away from the way her heart lurched at the seemingly innocuous question and continued to lurch with growing alarm every time she screamed in his arms. Every time his fingers lingered on her face, a look of faint bewilderment in his eyes as he watched her, then tumbled her into another mind-bending climax.

'I'd hoped you'd be done with this foolishness and be back home by now. Instead, you call with this news?' her mother demanded now, bringing Amelie tumbling back to earth and the reality that with morning always came the reminder that she still existed within the cyclone of a family feud.

'What I said before hasn't changed. We need to face reality.'

'But why does our reality have to involve *them*? Of all possible business partners, Amelie! You had to choose them?'

She didn't have the heart to say she hadn't *chosen* Atu's attention—that it had been the other way around. Then her mind flew back to last night and the hours that had followed. The sublime pleasure. The revelations of her own passion.

The things they'd done to each other!

It was a good thing she'd decided which way she was leaning with Atu's resort proposal while he was away in Kuala Lumpur, even though she hadn't yet informed him of her decision. Otherwise she would have had a hard time believing the transcendental sex hadn't swayed her.

She squeezed her eyes shut, blocking out the stunning view as she tried to refocus, tried to stem the pain as she reasoned with her mother.

'Isn't it better to deal with the devil you know?' she asked, echoing Atu's words.

'No, it's not,' her mother replied sharply. 'You're all I have left, Amelie. And I'm sad that you would break my heart this way.'

'Maa—' She flinched as the line went dead.

She told herself her mother needed time to come to terms with what was happening. That in this case the end would justify the means.

But Amelie couldn't stop the deep wave of despair that washed over her. Because even if she was making this decision with her head, and not her heart, she couldn't completely rule out the possibility that her heart was caught somewhere in the growing turmoil.

Atu stopped in her doorway, that feeling of protectiveness rising in him again when he caught the flash of pain in her eyes as she hung up.

'What's wrong?'

Her gaze veered from his and she tossed her phone onto the bed. He fought the urge to cross the room, pull her into his arms. One of many compulsive reactions that took him by constant surprise. It was almost as if his willpower had taken a permanent leave of absence around Amelie.

'I called home to check in with Maria. And to talk to my mother,' she replied, her voice subdued.

He didn't need a play-by-play to know who'd caused the anguish etched on her face. *He* still felt echoes of a similar emotion after his latest call with his father.

They hadn't discussed their family since the night he'd thrown the vault wide open. A part of him wanted to keep the vault shut on his own feelings, spurred him on to keep that condition in place. And yet he couldn't stop himself from speaking.

'Change isn't always comfortable. If this is a family legacy she truly wants to nurture and build, then she needs to think about your wishes—not just what she wants. And not what your father and sister would have wanted.'

She flinched and he felt a flash of guilt. But he stood resolute. For some reason getting her onside had now become *vital*. Her passion, her dedication—hell, even her stubbornness—were traits he found admirable.

And not just in the boardroom.

Discovering Amelie was passionate in every area of her life only fed the ravening hunger inside him.

'You want me to go to war with my own mother?' she asked.

He wasn't aware he'd moved until the scent of her perfume teased his nostrils. Until the sweet bow of her lips was only a few tempting inches away.

'I want you to fight for what you want.'

'And if I lose?'

Her voice trembled and he experienced that flash of guilt again. But this time a stronger wave of protectiveness rushed in along with it.

He clenched his gut against letting that sensation linger. Those were dangerous, life-altering emotions, similar to those his brother had felt before everything had turned to ash. He needed to leave emotion out of it.

And yet weren't the emotions Amelie expressed so fervently the very thing that drew him like a moth to a flame?

And how did that work out for the moth?

He suppressed a grim smile at the dark reminder.

'If you lose, then you'll know one way or the other, instead of merely existing in a half-life.'

She inhaled sharply, the shards of pain she tried so valiantly to hide darting all over her beautiful face. 'You think I've been living a half-life?'

'I think you have reserves of potential you're holding yourself back from exploring,' he answered.

'So you're the black sheep and I'm the forgotten daughter who can't get anything right?'

Fury rumbled through him. 'Did she say that to you?'

'Until today she's tolerated my running of the resort. Losing my father so soon after my sister... She hasn't coped very well.'

'You mean she expects you to be the perfect daughter but has abandoned any pretence of being a parent?' His indictment came out harsher than he'd meant it, but he didn't take back the words.

Again, she gave a pitiful shrug. 'Just now...she said I'd broken her heart.'

He clenched his teeth. Then, unable to resist, he tilted her face up to his. 'Put that out of your mind, Amelie. Live your life. If the path you choose causes her heartache, then you'll just have to reconcile yourself with it. We all have to live with our choices. Don't bury yourself in her needs.'

It struck him hard then that the resort was the last thing on his mind. He wanted her to thrive, full stop. The thought of Amelie being diminished in any way troubled him.

Her eyes grew suspiciously wet and Atu wanted to kick himself. But the tears never came. She worried at her bottom lip with her teeth, making him groan inwardly. Then she squared her shoulders and nodded.

He wasn't exactly sure why her bravery sent a dart of pleasure through him, nor was he certain why ensuring she wasn't sad felt so important. Perhaps he was simply weary of the heavy cloak of retribution he'd felt bound to bear.

Whatever...

'What about you?' she asked.

'What?'

'You just told me to live my life. What about you? Are you going to keep butting heads with your father for the rest of your life?'

He tensed, conflicted over whether or not to tell her that his father didn't have much time left, so that wouldn't be a problem for much longer. He was unprepared for the wave of despair that swept over him. Was he going to let another opportunity pass without clearing the air? Despite their volatile relationship, would he be able to live with himself?

'Atu?'

'He's sick,' he confessed gruffly. 'He likes to

pretend he's invincible, but the doctors don't hold out much hope.'

She gasped, sympathy filling her eyes. 'What? How…? When?'

'A while. He ignored the doctors' advice about his heart. Now it's too late.'

Her throat moved in a swallow. 'I… For what it's worth, I'm sorry.'

It was worth a lot. Much more than he wanted to admit. At every turn she surprised him. Now with her generosity towards the man who was intent on decimating her family as a last act from his deathbed.

It was almost enough to provoke *emotions* in Atu. If he believed in them.

To alleviate the unnerving emptiness triggered by thoughts of his dying father, he stepped closer, tugged her into his arms and sealed his mouth to hers the way he'd been dying to do since he entered the room.

When he lifted his head, he was smugly pleased to see her desire-glazed eyes. He should have taken the win, but apparently the dam he'd breached wasn't enough, and he found himself wading further into that emotion pool.

'Any particular reason she accused you of breaking her heart?'

Her fan-shaped lashes swept down as she gathered herself. When she lifted her gaze, the shadows of pain had receded, replaced by the passionate determination that had drawn him since he'd first become aware of the little sister of the woman his brother had lost his head over.

'I told her I was thinking of partnering with you on the resort project.'

His heart leapt even while his eyes narrowed. 'You're *thinking*?'

'I didn't see the need to tell her that I'd already decided to say yes to you,' she murmured.

He allowed himself a smile that probably reeked of triumph. 'Good to hear. You'll find that I'm a worthwhile ally.'

They were officially working partners. And sexual partners for the time being. Both his expectations had finally been realised.

So why did he feel as if time was already slipping through his fingers?

Amelie followed the path down to the private beach attached to Atu's villa four days later, smiling at the maid who set a tray of cold drinks down and promptly made herself scarce.

Once she'd greenlit the project, they'd flown to Kuala Lumpur to meet with Atu's team. Now new blueprints were being drawn up, with a heavier emphasis on eco-lodges and greater sustainability.

She'd been reviewing the contracts when a maid had informed her that Mr Quayson required her presence on the beach, giving her the perfect excuse not to think about the way her heart continued to squeeze every time she recalled the harrowing conversation with her mother.

Her mother might never come around. But Amelie had to keep reminding herself that what she was doing was perpetuating a bigger legacy—not just for the small family she had left, but for her community. Perhaps for the children she might have one day.

That constant reminder was what kept her from sliding into despair over her mother's cutting disapproval.

Sipping her drink now, she approached a curtained cabana set up on a wide platform between two palm trees. Stepping inside, she stopped at the sight of Atu, leaning against a massage bed.

'Um…what's happening?'

He smiled, and her stomach performed a breath-snagging flip-flop.

'You wanted a massage. I'm here to deliver.'

'Is this why my appointment with Assan keeps getting mysteriously rescheduled?'

He shrugged. 'I can top what he offers. If not, he'll be made available to you at the very next opportunity.'

Her smile turned into a laugh. 'Competitive, much?'

He winked at her. 'Always.'

She found herself smiling, then bursting into laughter. His eyes widened fractionally, making her self-conscious. 'I think I might try Assan anyway, so I can compare it to you.'

Humour vanished from his face. 'I despise the thought of another man touching you—even professionally. If that makes me a primitive bastard, then so be it,' he said, without a hint of apology.

She was an independent forward-thinking woman. A strong feminist. Yet the growly possessiveness in his voice made her knees weak and heat dampen her core in a way that would have shocked her only a little while ago.

But hadn't all her previous notions when it came to living her life fallen by the wayside where Atu was involved?

Was this how her sister had felt about Fiifi? Had she been driven into taking drastic decisions, triggering the tragic events that had shattered their families?

He frowned. 'What's wrong?'

She shook her head. 'Nothing.'

He took her chin in his large, firm hand. 'Tell me,' he insisted.

'All the no-go areas we agreed not to touch on seem to be rushing at us.'

His eyes narrowed. 'Family again?'

She nodded. 'My sister. Your brother.'

Tension rippled through his jaw and his hand dropped from her chin. 'What about them?'

'Did you have any idea that things were so... *charged* between them?'

His bark of laughter was laced with bitterness. 'Everyone knew that your sister was driving Fiifi to insanity, Amelie.'

A plaintive inner voice demanded to know why she'd brought this up now. But she glared through her distress. 'Excuse me?'

'Don't pretend you don't know what I'm talking about.'

She'd heard the accusations enough times to know their families blamed each other for the deaths of their firstborns. Somehow she hadn't considered that Atu shared that sentiment.

She jumped from the massage table, her throat tight with prickling tears.

'Where do you think you're going?' he demanded.

'I don't think I can bear you to touch me right now.'

'Because you don't like hearing the truth?'

'The truth according to you. I have a different version of events. One where it was *your* brother who played games with *my* sister and drove her to act out of character.'

He folded his arms, his jaw rippling. 'Whatever was pushing them, they escalated a dangerous situation by driving drunk and then crashing. Perhaps we should leave that particular episode where it belongs.'

'But how can we? Isn't the past that lies between us the reason you've dragged me across the world?'

Something gleamed at the back of his eyes—perhaps a dart of hurt at her indictment. Her heart twanged uncomfortably, but before she could speak, he let out a heavy sigh.

'Fiifi was used to getting what he wanted when he wanted. He'd never known true denial. Everything he wished for, he got.'

'Until he met my sister?' Amelie knew how

long Fiifi had pursued Esi before she'd even agreed to go out with him.

Atu shrugged. 'She was a challenge, according to him.'

She bristled at the statement. 'One he had to conquer by any means?'

A shroud of pain drifted over his face. Then his features hardened. 'I'd like to think neither of them wanted that eventual outcome.'

'But he pushed and he pushed, until...'

Atu's eyes narrowed. 'If you're suggesting it's a Quayson trait, you're wrong.'

'Why? Because love isn't a characteristic of the Quaysons, as you claim?' She shook her head. 'Whether you want to admit it or not, *passion* and *love* drove them. Granted, it wasn't neat and clinical, like you think relationships should be.'

His jaw gritted. 'This isn't about how I feel—'

'For once, you're right. This is about *them*. I think it's time we admit that whether or not my sister was driving your brother to distraction, or whether or not she was giving him a hard time because she didn't have his attention when she demanded it, doesn't matter any more. They were adults—responsible for their actions. And, as tragic as those actions were, blaming them, or ourselves, won't change anything. We can't change the past.'

'Perhaps not—but we can use it to inform us.'

'Of what, exactly? That love doesn't exist?' Before he could respond, she pushed on. 'This from the man who returned to his father's bedside despite everything?'

He stiffened. 'What are you trying to say?'

'That you *feel*, Atu. You try to hide it, but you feel everything—perhaps even more than most.'

He stiffened even further. 'I wouldn't lay bets on that if I were you.'

'No? Then answer me this. Deep down, do you believe, had your brother lived, that you could've talked him out of the way he felt about my sister?'

His brows clamped together. Then his lips thinned. But in his eyes she saw a wavering—the first sign that Atu was uncertain about something.

She wasn't sure where she found the utter conviction to place her hand on his chest and lock eyes with him. 'You don't, do you? You can't prove to me that he didn't love her.'

'No, I can't. There was an intensity about what he felt for your sister...'

She fought a smile at the almost disgruntled admission, even while she felt a punch of sadness that he couldn't utter the word *love*. 'Okay. So we're going to let this go. Right here and now.'

Amelie could have sworn that swiftly behind the rebellion that blazed through his eyes came relief, but both emotions disappeared in seconds.

'Just like that?' he asked, but again, the heaviness from moments before had lightened. As if a burden had been lifted.

She shrugged, barely able to contain the punch of emotion reeling through her. She'd never stopped to think how her sister would have felt about this. Now she had, she knew Esi would never have wanted this enmity on her behalf. Not when she'd openly rebelled, choosing Fiifi despite their families' fierce disapproval.

'We have enough things to butt heads over. I'm choosing this not to be one of them.'

After an eternity, he nodded. 'Very well.'

Relief and a profound serenity swelled through her. But when she started to pull away, he held on. 'Where do you think you're going?'

'Oh… I thought…'

Her words trailed away as she saw heat slowly gathering in his eyes. 'The massage is still happening. Unless you want to butt heads about that?'

Answering heat collected low in her belly, and

her fingers curled into his chest. 'No, I don't,' she said breathlessly.

'Take off your clothes,' he growled.

Amelie was thankful she didn't have to dwell on the enormous ghost they'd just laid to rest. Because if she did, then she might start to wonder whether there were other battles they could conquer. Other miracles they could create.

Sheer possibility made her hands tremble as she reached for the ties securing her sundress. It fell from her shoulders, leaving her in a white bikini.

Her breath caught when he turned to face her, subjecting her to a long, lingering scrutiny that ended with a tight look of hunger on his face.

After another age, his gaze dropped to her bikini top. 'That needs to come off too,' he said, his deep voice gravel-rough.

Unlike her session with him, this massage wasn't happening with any semblance of professionalism. Atu was touching her because he wanted to. And she was allowing it because the need to have his hands on her invalidated any common sense that should've dictated her actions.

She wanted this. Full stop.

'Now, Amelie…' he growled, implacable command in his eyes.

Her trembling hands rose to the back of her neck, pulled on the strings. She caught the cups before they fell free and then, heat suffusing her whole body, arranged herself on the table before discarding the top.

Behind her, he made a rough sound. She was too afraid to look. Too afraid to confront the depths of emotions rampaging through her.

Again unlike her, he didn't choose meditative stress-relief music. Instead, the strains of soulful jazz permeated the room, making her groan under her breath.

Was she surprised that he knew what that kind of music did to her? That some of her most memorable moments had involved dancing carefree to the music she loved?

She swallowed hard when the scent of hemp oil teased her nostrils. Unable to resist, she turned her head, watched him flick the top of a small bottle and dribble golden liquid into his palm. Still pinning her with his fierce gaze, he slowly rubbed his hands together, then slid them firmly over her shoulders.

She couldn't voice anything besides his name, because he intuited her every need. His firm hands paid exquisite attention to her fingers, palms and arms until she sighed with pleasure. Then he moved to her legs.

She hadn't wasted any time wondering if he would be a decent masseur. Atu was exceptional. And, just like everything else he did, its effect frightened her a little.

'Deep breaths, Amelie. No use fighting this. Let it go.'

She'd instinctively tensed at her thoughts, but somehow she doubted he was talking about the massage.

She was in this thing for the foreseeable future.

The most vital thing was not to hand over anything else that was precious to her.

Like her heart.

Even if she had a stomach-hollowing suspicion it might be too late…

Those moments in the cabana set the tone for their remaining days in Malaysia, and then continued into the next week when they flew to Malta.

Maria was holding the fort admirably back home, and until she signed on the dotted line, Amelie had decided to keep the news just to her. Her manager had been thrilled, and the offer from Atu of a bigger role in the new resort had brought even more enthusiasm.

Perhaps that was why Amelie had gone a little crazy and agreed to Atu's suggestion to extend their trip by another two weeks.

Staying away longer also meant she didn't have to face her mother just yet. Amelie hoped by the time she did she would also have the completed blueprints that she was sure would make the vision she'd chosen more palatable to her mother.

If Q Cove was a sublime sanctuary, nestled between the beach and the rainforest, Q Valletta was a perfect haven, poised above the culturally vibrant Mediterranean city. Atu's signature luxury was everywhere, and every guest's wish was a phone call or an attentive staff member away.

They'd spent an extra week in Malaysia because she hadn't been able to tear herself away from the resort. And although she was exhausted when they landed in Malta, on account of Atu's insatiable demands upon her body during the flight from Malaysia, she threw herself into exploring the hotel and the city the moment she was rested.

Their week passed in a blur of resort-planning, sightseeing and sublime sex—the kind she was sure skilled authors rhapsodised about.

Then, on their last day, her life began to unravel.

Although she didn't know it, it had started with an email from Maria the night before.

Call me when you have a minute, please?

She'd missed seeing it because they'd been at a VIP-only nightclub until the early hours, and then had fallen into bed after frenzied lovemaking against the wall on their return.

And this morning Amelie hadn't surfaced until gone ten a.m., only to rush to the bathroom with the kind of nausea that mocked her for overindulging in oysters the night before.

Now, leaving the bathroom, she let her mind idly tumble through dates and monthly cycles, only to freeze in the middle of the suite.

A whole week had passed since her period should have made an appearance!

She swayed as the connotations hit her—hard.

Luckily, Atu had risen earlier, to meet with his resort manager before they headed for the airport, so she was alone.

She stumbled back to bed, frantically grabbing her phone to double-check dates, dismissing the flashing email icon.

She felt a cold wave wash over her as her suspicions were confirmed.

Shocked, she couldn't stop every possible worst-case scenario from crashing through her head—the worst being her mother's voice, condemning her to eternity.

Then her spine stiffened, and her shaky hand drifted over her flat stomach.

These past few weeks had shown her how different things could be, hadn't they? *If* she was carrying the Quayson-Hayford heir, surely it wouldn't be the end of the world?

Sharp on the heels of that thought, she felt her spirits plummet.

Yes, it would be. Atu didn't believe in love. He believed in business arrangements, not arrangements of the heart. Whereas somewhere in the heady circus of the last month she'd lost her heart to her family's sworn enemy.

But he wasn't her enemy any longer.

He was the man she'd spun dreams around as a starry-eyed teenager, and he was the man she'd given her heart to as a self-aware woman.

But still… *A baby.*

The idea saturated her, and with it came a quiet awe which grew and grew and made her shattering heart swell with a different emotion. An emotion that affirmed to her that she would love this child with every fibre of her being. That she would not play favourites the way her parents and Atu's parents had done.

She'd forged a new beginning for herself in Malaysia. This would be another wonderful new beginning. A challenge she would rise to.

The urge to know for sure one way or the other grew too large to contain. They weren't due at the airport for another two hours. Rising, she threw on her clothes, grabbed her phone and headed for the door—abruptly stopping when the butler assigned to their suite appeared from the kitchen.

'May I help you with anything, madam?'

'Can you let Mr Quayson know I've stepped out for a few minutes? I'll be back shortly.'

He nodded, executing the courteous little bow she suspected was ingrained into every Quayson Group staff member.

The wild, foolish hope that this would be a new beginning for her family and Atu's family grew larger as she followed the concierge's directions to the pharmacy two streets away. Snatching a pregnancy test off the counter, she completed her purchase and was back in the suite within ten minutes.

In the bathroom, she stared at herself in the

mirror, the notion that her life might be about to change yet again dousing her in chills.

You can do this.

Willing her fingers to stop shaking, she pulled out the test.

But no amount of reaffirming words could make her stay calm as the flashing word confirmed her new reality.

She was pregnant with Atu's child.

CHAPTER TEN

THE KNOCK ON the bathroom door made her jump.

'Amelie?'

She bit her lip, unsure whether her voice would hold if she tried to answer. Her heart ramming hard against her ribs, she stumbled to the door and turned the handle.

'Amelie, are you okay?' Atu's brow was knotted in concern, his gaze raking over her face. 'The butler says you haven't had breakfast yet. Is there something—?'

He froze, his gaze latching on the testing kit sitting on the counter before widening on her face.

She knew the exact moment the truth hit him. Heard his sharp inhalation as his gaze fixed on hers, searching wildly. And it was because she was staring directly at him, feverishly reading his expression the way he did to her when they were in bed, that she saw his rejection of the truth she'd just dropped into his lap.

When he compounded it by taking a stunned step backwards, everything inside her froze.

She wouldn't have thought it possible that her world could go from hopeful and awe-filled to desolate within three heartbeats. And yet she felt fiercely proud of herself as she straightened from wilting against the doorjamb and walked past him into the suite.

'You don't need to worry. I'm not about to hit you with a paternity suit. The child will be my responsibility alone.'

'Excuse me?' His voice was iceberg-cold.

'You heard me.' She glanced over her shoulder, even now attempting to see if she'd been mistaken, if a small part of him shared this quiet happiness moving inside her.

But no.

If anything, his features had grown more granite-like. He was an imposing pillar, his arms folded across his chest and rejection stamped into every inch of his being.

'I imagine men in your position are hit with demands like that every other week?' she said, attempting to infuse a casualness she didn't feel into her voice. It fell far short. 'I'm just saying you don't need to worry about anything like that with me.'

His eyes narrowed. 'Don't need to worry about...?' He shook his head as if he couldn't quite believe what was happening. 'Are you serious?'

She wanted to laugh, but suspected it would

come out as a totally different, unwanted sound, so she clamped her mouth shut.

'You tell me you're pregnant... No, wait... I won't make the mistake of assuming. *Are* you pregnant with my child, Amelie?'

She whirled around then and felt something wither inside her. All along, part of her had known her stupid dreams were based on wishful thinking. Dear God, he couldn't have spelt it out any more plainly for her, and yet she'd still lost her heart to this man.

Clearly tired of waiting for her answer, he stalked into the bathroom and stood frozen, staring down at the stick proclaiming that he was about to become a father.

Was that a shudder going through him?

She couldn't look any more, so she turned, entered the dressing room and started packing her case.

Minutes passed in scalding silence. Then she heard him approach.

'When did you know?' he breathed, his voice barely a rumble.

'Does it matter?' That compulsion struck again, dragging her gaze to him. 'I promise I didn't trick you.'

His face darkened and a tic pulsed in his jaw.

'Don't put words in my mouth. I have a right to know when my child was conceived, do I not?'

This time she couldn't stop the laughter that seared her throat. 'I can't give you a time and date, Atu.'

He exhaled noisily, one hand dragging over his nape as he paced to where she stood. 'How do you feel?' he asked gruffly.

Something inside her—a hard knot she realised she had formed to protect her from her shattered dreams—threatened to dissolve, but she held tightly on to it. Asking after her health didn't mean he was ready to embrace fatherhood. He'd do the same for the butler, or any of his thousands of employees.

'I feel fine. I thought I was having a reaction to the oysters from last night, but it turns out…'

He held her gaze for a moment, his lips pursed, and then he nodded.

For a full minute they regarded each other in stony silence, the *joie de vivre* they'd basked in for the past month gone for ever.

Unable to stand it any longer, she turned and continued her packing.

'Leave that. Let the butler take care of it,' he instructed.

She shook her head. 'No. I'm done.'

A vice tightened around her heart as the words echoed in her head.

She wasn't the one who was done. The tension gripping his shoulders announced that *he* was done.

And over the next hour, as they were chauffeured to the airport, Amelie's worst fears came true. He'd barely said a word to her, his tablet his sole focus as they transferred from car to jet.

The moment they took off, he rose. 'If you're still feeling unwell, I suggest you go and lie down in the bedroom.'

Bitterness soured her mouth. 'So we're not going to talk about this?'

He shook his head. 'You're pregnant with my child. That's a definitive situation if ever there was one, isn't it?'

Desolation threatened to sweep over her again, but she summoned fury instead. 'You make me sound like a hopeless, inevitable cause.'

He slanted her a grim smile. 'No, Amelie. What you are is pregnant, and the consequences of that can only go one way.'

She gasped. 'If you think I'm going to get rid—'

'Let me stop you right there. You're carrying my heir. While the news may have come as a shock, know that I intend to claim my flesh and blood in the fullest possible sense.'

He was saying the words she yearned to hear. But every drawn line on his face, every ragged breath he took, the distance he'd placed between them, told her this was far from a happy outcome for him.

So she let his words drift over her, accepting that this was a moment for retreat and regrouping.

Because a Quayson was threatening to claim what was hers. *Again.*

She'd handed over her resort, her soul and, most foolishly, her heart.

Her baby was hers to keep. Because not for one moment would she subject it to the same brutal rejection she'd suffered.

She stood, not looking back as she made her way down the length of the plane to the bedroom suite. It was only after she'd shut and locked the door behind her that she collapsed into a heap on the bed.

For the next hour she let her emotions free, sobbing into the pillows until she was drained. Then, against her will, she fell asleep.

Once again Atu paced the confines of his plane's conference room—only this time, neither anger nor frustration dogged his steps.

There was shock—although, in hindsight, the

passionate frenzy with which he and Amelie had explored each other these past few weeks should have given him a heads-up—and dread. Because he knew next to nothing about babies except that they were completely helpless and sponges for whatever emotion was focused on them.

And that drew the worst sentiment—a debilitating sense of *fear*. Yes, he, the all-powerful Quayson who hadn't hesitated to risk being disowned, despite his father's threats, who'd borne the shame and guilt of knowing he'd let his brother down without buckling, was terrified of this new challenge.

Because it was a sacred challenge.

What would his brother advise if he were alive?

Seize the moment?

Live your life?

Wasn't that what his brother had been trying to do? Hell, hadn't he shrugged and recommended Atu do the same if that was what he wanted, and to hell with the consequences? What was life worth if the only thing he'd let matter to him was striking the next deal?

Hadn't this past month shown him a stark difference from the life he'd led before Amelie? Those feelings of protectiveness and possessiveness…that need to be close to Amelie when logic dictated he pull back... They'd stubbornly lingered, right alongside their insane chemistry, which had grown and morphed until it seemed to have attained a life of its own.

A life that bore no signs of diminishing.

A life full of...*feelings.*

He passed a hand over his rough stubble and wasn't surprised to feel it trembling.

A baby. *His child.*

He'd meant it when he'd stated his intention to claim it. But then what? He was great at instructing a team of talented architects to draft blueprints for his masterpieces. But the stark realisation that he had no one to rely on as a father but himself made his insides congeal.

Because what tools did he have to fashion the most important blueprint of all?

How could he claim his child when he had no idea how to be a good father?

Amelie awoke at a knock from one of the attendants, telling her they were about to land in Accra. Realising she'd slept through the whole flight stunned her. Straightening her clothes, she secured herself in the armchair next to the bed and fought the fresh tears that rose.

She'd left here over a month ago, confused and

desolate at the turn of events in her life. Then, for a few exhilarating weeks, she'd believed her life could be turned around. Yet now here she was, even more devastated and desolate than before.

She'd dared to love. And she was about to lose.

When the plane drew to a halt, she rose from the armchair, freezing when Atu appeared in the doorway.

'Did you sleep?' His voice was still cool.

She nodded. Then her throat dried as his gaze drifted over her, lingering on her belly for several charged moments.

'Come. The car's waiting.'

She went to retrieve her handbag from the bedside table, then jolted as several pings sounded in the quiet cabin.

Grabbing her phone, she stared down at the screen.

Thirteen messages from Maria.

Aware of Atu waiting impatiently by the door, she shoved the phone back into her bag and slung it over her shoulder.

She would check them in the car.

The same sleek town car that had driven her from Saltpond waited on the tarmac. She barely registered the short drive from the airport to Atu's home in Quayson Hills. She tried not to be awed by the sense of her insignificance in the face of the power and might of a man who even had an exclusive city enclave named after him.

'I intend to claim my child in the fullest possible sense...'

Amelie straightened her spine. She'd vowed not to let herself be cowed by him. She wasn't about to start now.

'Why are we going to your house?'

'Because we need to talk.'

'Haven't we done that already?'

Piercing eyes met hers. 'Hardly. You announced you were pregnant with my child and then proceeded to shut me out. I, in turn, made a claim on it. Unless you've had a profound change of mind, I think we need to arrive at some compromise.'

Compromise.

Not exactly business-speak, but not warm and fuzzy either.

'Atu...'

'I called my private doctor from the plane. He can see us tomorrow, if that's acceptable to you?' he said gruffly.

That traitorous place inside her softened some more. Because she already loved this baby more than anything, she couldn't fault Atu for taking time out of his busy life to ensure its well-being.

But as the driver pulled up the long driveway and stopped in front of a jaw-dropping mansion, the full impact of his words registered.

'Tomorrow morning? Does that mean you expect me to sleep here? With you?' She ignored the harsh tautening of his face, panic flaring inside her. 'Because—'

'I have a dozen guest rooms, Amelie. You can take your pick if the thought of sharing a bed with me appals you now,' he returned tightly.

He flung the door open before she could respond, then held out a hand to help her out.

Aware of the driver, and of the two members of his staff unloading their luggage, Amelie pursed her lips.

The interior of Atu's house was as stunning as the outside, but besides a vague perception of soaring ceilings, exquisite art and plush carpeting, she barely registered it. Her sole focus was the broad-shouldered man leading her into a vast living room.

Going to a well-appointed bar, he poured her a glass of mineral water, then a shot of whisky for himself.

She sat and he remained standing, his crystal glass clutched in one hand.

'I will be in this child's life. Full-time. I want that to be a given before we go any further.'

This child. Not her. The vice squeezed so tight around her heart she was stunned it could still beat.

'It's your turn to tell me what you want,' he said.

Despair shuddered through her, and the thudding of her heart was almost a dirge for every shattered hope.

'I want...' She shook her head. 'What I want is impossible for you. I know that now.'

His lips parted, as if he wanted to refute that, but his phone rang just then. He ignored it, his eyes fixed on her.

'Aren't you going to get that?' she asked.

He reached for his phone at the same time as his doorbell pealed, followed seconds later by urgent footsteps.

Amelie looked up in surprise as Ekow, Atu's younger brother, strode into the living room. The brothers were of equal height, and he bore the same unmistakable Quayson swagger, the same chiselled good looks. And right now the same tight-jawed expression Atu was wearing.

His gaze rested on her for a moment, his lack of surprise making her wonder if Atu had mentioned their affair. But then she recalled the dozens of guests who'd seen them together at her resort. By now everyone in the country knew they'd been together for the last few weeks.

'It's good to see you, Amelie.'

Since she wasn't sure if she believed him, she merely nodded.

He turned to his brother. 'I need to talk to you.'

Atu frowned. 'It'll have to wait. We're in the middle of...' His words trailed off as his brother shook his head.

'It can't. Dad's in hospital. His doctors think he's got pneumonia.'

The slash of pain and worry on Atu's face made her heart lurch. Those were real human emotions. So why didn't he feel any for her? Was she truly as lacking to everyone as her mother found her?

She wrapped her hands around the handbag in her lap to disguise their trembling and felt her phone vibrate again.

The brothers were speaking in low, urgent voices, so she rose, walked a few feet away and pressed the phone to her ear.

For several moments she couldn't quite make out what Maria was saying. When she did, every atom in her body froze.

'Amelie? What is it?'

She stared in horror at Atu, the enormity of her gullibility threatening to drown her. 'My God... This was all an elaborate plan, wasn't it?'

'What are you talking about?' he bit out.

'You tricked me into leaving the country so... so you could do this!'

His already thunderous brow darkened even further. 'I've no idea what you're talking about.'

'Pull the other one, Atu.'

A tic appeared at his temple. 'Please do me the courtesy of telling me what I've done before lobbing accusations at me.'

'You *know* what you've done, you bastard. You made sure I was on the other side of the world and then got your bank to buy up my business loan. You couldn't even be bothered to give me the partnership we agreed on, could you?' Her prickling eyes swung to his brother. 'I'm guessing you were in on this too? You don't seem surprised to see me here.'

Atu's jaw worked furiously. 'Amelie, don't...'

'Don't what? Call you the slimy bastard you truly are?'

'Watch your tongue,' he warned silkily.

She didn't care what audience they had. Hell, she wanted to scream at him from the top of her lungs. But she had a new life growing inside her—one that absolutely required she keep a level head.

'I'll fight you. Mark my words. I will fight you until I have no breath left.'

His face twisted.

Only yesterday she might have fooled herself into thinking that was a display of anguish. She knew better now. He had no feelings for her. And as she watched, he dragged himself back under furious control.

'Whatever you think I've done, you're wrong.'

'Save it, Atu. Your bank bought up my business loan two weeks ago. This morning your lawyers are calling it in. They've given me forty-eight hours to pay up or they'll take my resort. You were always going to go ahead with or without my agreement, weren't you?'

For a fraction of a second his face slackened with shock. Then he turned to his brother. Ekow's subtle shake of the head stopped whatever question he'd been about to ask.

He turned back to her. 'I need to go. But we're not done talking. I'll be back in a few hours. We can finish then.'

Amelie stepped forward, anger threatening to take over. 'Perhaps you didn't hear me? I want nothing to do with you. And I'm most definitely not staying here.' Her grip tightened on her phone. 'And, just so we're clear, our agreement is off. If you set foot in my resort, I'll call the authorities.'

His head went back as if he'd been struck. 'Are you sure you want to go down that road? After all, if what you're saying is true, then the resort will be mine in two days anyway.'

She wanted to cry. No doubt it was the pregnancy hormones at work. Instead, she clenched her jaw until the sensation receded. Then, to her eternal glee, she managed to summon a smile. 'It's mine until then. And you're not welcome there.'

Whirling around, she hurried out of the living room, just in time to see a maid rolling her suitcase towards the stairs.

'Wait!'

She hurried over to grab it just as Atu lunged forward, as if to stop her. At the last moment, he balled his fists.

'This isn't over, Amelie...' he breathed. 'Far from it.'

Her hand tightened around the handle of her suitcase and, desperately, she took a few more steps away from him.

He followed her outside, where the driver still

stood beside the car. 'Take Miss Hayford wherever she wants to go.'

And because it was the quickest way to get away from the man who'd completely decimated her life, she slid back into the car, averting her gaze from him as he stood watching her being driven away.

The sight of his father, hooked up to half a dozen machines, reduced to a husk when just over a month ago, despite the fact he'd been ill, he had retained layers of his former power and vibrancy, shocked Atu to his core.

He remained frozen in the doorway of the private hospital suite until his mother looked up. 'Aren't you coming in?'

His father's thin lids flickered. Then he opened his eyes. 'Ah, the black sheep graces us with his presence…'

His mother rose, brushed a kiss on her husband's jaw before crossing over to do the same to Atu. 'I'll leave you two alone.'

'I sent you to do a job—not to succumb to the witchcraft of another Hayford temptress,' his father snarled the moment his mother shut the door behind her.

Fury spiked through him, but he kept it leashed. 'Do not call her that.'

'Why not? The other one led your brother astray!'

'She didn't. He loved her. And she loved him back.'

He was fairly sure he understood the emotion now. Because tonight he'd felt the same desperation Fiifi had displayed. That need to burn the world to the ground just for a chance to see Amelie smile at him again. To have her wrap her arms around his neck and stare up at him with those beautiful eyes.

But with another cruel Quayson act, he'd lost any chance with her. 'Why did you do it?' he asked.

His father didn't bother pretending ignorance. 'Because you'd gone soft. Because they need to pay for taking my son from me.'

'No, Dad. You did that all on your own.'

His father's lips twisted. 'So, what? You're going to give it all up for love too? Just like your brother?'

Astonishment froze his spine. 'You knew?'

'Of course I knew! Why do you think I wanted you around to talk some sense into him? But you couldn't even do that, could you?'

'Yes, I failed at that. But *you* failed us all. Don't worry—since you want me in charge so badly, I will take control of this family. But I'll do things differently. As of today, this campaign of retribution is over. Wherever he is, I know that's what Fiifi would want. I plan to earn his forgiveness by doing that, at least.'

Shock widened his father's eyes. Then fury replaced it. '*I* will never forgive you,' his father rasped, just as the machines started wailing.

It took a monumental effort for Atu to swallow the rock lodged in his throat. 'I know. And I can't change that. But, for what it's worth, I forgive *you.*'

CHAPTER ELEVEN

AMELIE LET HERSELF into her home two hours later, her eyes gritty with unshed tears and her insides numb. She'd hoped to feel a modicum of joy at being home, but even now every treacherous bone in her body wanted to be back with Atu—*before* she'd discovered the depth of his betrayal.

But she would wean herself of that, somehow. Just as she'd—

'You're home at last.'

She froze in the living room doorway, her gaze clashing with her mother's. Despite the lateness of the hour, her mother was fully dressed. And the gaze she fixed on Amelie was firm and direct.

Unable to stop herself, she let her hand fly to her flat belly. The belly she'd been caressing all through the journey from Accra. Despite the devastating unravelling of her hopes and dreams, she felt a fierce protectiveness and love for the child growing inside her. She had vowed that nothing and no one would stop her from being the best mother she could be. Not even her own mother.

'What are you doing up, Maa?' she asked, her heart firmly lodged in her throat. After what she'd been through with Atu, she couldn't take further censure or rejection. Couldn't even dredge up any hope for the acceptance her heart craved.

'You were supposed to be gone for only two weeks,' her mother said.

'I know.' She swallowed, and braced herself for what she needed to say. 'Maa, I need to tell you something...'

Priscilla Hayford nodded, a knowing light shifting away the traces of sorrow, replacing it with a glimpse of the mother Amelie had used to know. 'You love him, don't you? The Quayson boy?'

Amelie's chin quivered, seismic emotion shaking through her. 'Yes. Do...do you hate me?'

Shock filled her mother's eyes. '*Hate* you? Why would you think that?'

Her despondent shrug weighed a hundred tons. 'Because I'm a disappointment. Because I've betrayed our family. Because you said I was breaking your heart by going with him. You said—'

'Hush, child. No parent wants to be reminded of how they've failed their child. I'll have years to flay myself for that, believe me.'

Stunned, Amelie's mouth gaped. 'What?'

Her mother shook her head mournfully. 'When you didn't return two weeks ago, and Maria told me you'd extended your trip, I was terrified.'

'Maa—'

'No, it was the wake-up call I needed. The thought that I was losing you too… These past few weeks I've had nothing but time to think really hard about what I've done, Amelie. I've been forced to consider that maybe you didn't want to come back because there was nothing for you to come back for. Not even your mother—because I haven't been here for you, have I?'

Unable to lie, Amelie shook her head.

Her mother swallowed hard. 'Oh, my child. I'm so sorry.' Her voice broke as she held out her arms.

Amelie flew into them, greedily snatching at the affection she'd missed so terribly for most of her life. 'Oh, Maa.'

Her mother soothed her through her quiet sobs. 'I know I've been lost in grief. I know I've done a poor job of showing you how treasured you are. I promise I'll do better. Now, tell me what's happened.'

'Are you sure? It's not… I don't know if…'

Her mother drew back, her gaze drifting from the hand Amelie still splayed over her stomach to her face. 'Whatever it is, we'll get through it, child. You're home now, and I'm here for you. Now, tell me everything.'

With another sob spilling free, Amelie unburdened all the pain and devastation in her heart.

* * *

Atu walked along the beach, contemplating and discarding snippets of conversation as wave after wave of despair washed over him.

He'd checked into Amelie's resort last night, making sure his staff had booked him under a corporate name again. He'd taken her wishes seriously, even though technically his family bank owned the resort now.

Not that he planned on activating any of the repossession clauses.

He was the head of his family now, after all.

Another wave of despair passed over him, steeped in sorrow he doubted he would have felt only a few months ago.

Before her, he'd closed himself off, just so this level of pain wouldn't penetrate his armour. A few short weeks was all it had taken to crumble every brick of the foundations he'd erected around his heart.

Now he mourned his father, who'd passed away a week after their return, and he lived in a state of awed hope for the child he hoped to become a better father to than his own father had been to him.

But most important of all, his heart ached with

longing for the woman he'd fallen hopelessly in love with.

The woman who had refused every contact from him until he'd been forced to retreat.

Misery shuddered through him, and he realised he'd stopped on the edge of the boundary separating Amelie's house from her resort.

A figure drifted towards him. His heart lurched, then somersaulted, before hammering hard.

The person drew closer and his spirits dropped.

It wasn't Amelie.

But the unmistakable figure of her mother was hard to miss. She came towards him, her eyes narrowing as recognition sparked in a face so similar to that of the woman he loved.

'Atu?'

Despite the dark emotions swirling inside him, he summoned a dry smile. 'Yes, Auntie.'

Her face softened for a fractional moment. 'What do you want?'

His gaze drifted past her and up to Amelie's window.

Before he could voice the longing burning in his soul, she spoke again. 'Perhaps I should ask what took you so long?'

His gaze flew back to her. 'Why? Is she…?'

'Alive? Barely. Eating?' She shrugged. 'Only

for the sake of the child she carries. Is she wearing a look similar to the one on your face? Most definitely.'

The last was said with a bite of accusation that sent another shiver over him.

He hadn't seen or spoken to Amelie's mother in almost a decade, and yet beneath her shroud of grief he spotted in the older woman the formidable woman the daughter was turning out to be.

Several scenarios had unfolded in his brain of how he would conduct this meeting, but he hadn't factored in encountering the mother instead of the daughter.

Still, he thought grimly, he was fighting for his life. 'I want to see her,' he said.

'You can want all you like. My daughter does as she pleases.'

Was that a hint of pride in her voice? Before he could be certain, another figure drifted down the path leading to where they stood.

His heart started hammering wildly in his chest as he stared. This time it was Amelie.

He wasn't aware her mother had moved closer until she touched his arm. 'Tread carefully, son, but tread well. For the sake of my grandchild.'

His heart leapt at the words, but he barely

sensed her leave. Every scrap of his attention was pinned on Amelie.

She'd lost a little weight. Her face was drawn. But she looked breathtaking. Every sleepless night he'd spent reliving each moment of their four weeks together had done little justice to the real living and breathing woman in front of him.

'What do you want?' she asked.

He didn't answer for several moments, simply content to be drenched in the sound of her voice.

'I couldn't stay away. I know you wanted me to, but I couldn't.'

She wrapped her arms around her waist and Atu saw her shiver. As much as he was dying to rip off his shirt and cover her with it, he forced himself to stay still. But his eyes couldn't stop devouring her. Cataloguing every square inch of the body he adored more than life itself.

She gave a harsh laugh. 'You've done very well for two months. Why not for the rest of your life?'

'Because I won't make it.'

She inhaled sharply, and her gaze dropped from his as if she couldn't bear to look at him. She started to turn away. 'I can't do this.'

'Please.' The word shot out of him. 'I deserve every accusation you throw at me, but hear me out. I beg you.'

She paused, still half turned from him. His eager gaze drew down her body, lingering on her belly. His heart caught at the sight of the slight swell where his child grew.

He dragged his gaze back to her face, then summoned the words he didn't really want to speak. 'You heard my father passed away?'

Her lips pressed together and then she nodded. 'Yes. I'm sorry.'

He forced a shrug, but the lance of pain arrived anyway. 'I thought I'd feel nothing when the moment came. But nothing ever prepares you for that. Just like with Fiifi. It takes the legs from underneath you.'

Her face softened and she turned fully to face him once more. 'Yes, I know. Emotions are like that. They catch you when you least expect it.'

He nodded, a half-smile tugging at his lips. 'It's the darnedest thing… For so long I hated him for not loving me as much as he loved his firstborn son. But I came running the moment he said he needed me.'

'It's because he was your father. No matter what happens, every child wants their parents' love.'

Again, his gaze dropped to her belly, every cell in his body yearning for the child she carried. 'Amelie…'

'I'm fine. The baby is fine.'

He wasn't aware he was holding his breath until it exploded out of him. The hand he lifted to grip his nape trembled wildly against his skin. He remembered to nod, his scattered mind attempting to form more words when all he wanted to do was reach across the gap between them, drag her into his arms and never let go.

'I resented Fiifi for being the sole recipient of our father's love and respect, for being the favoured son. Sometimes he was cruel about it. Other times he was smug. But it was the pity I hated most.' He saw her lower lip tremble and he shook his head. 'This isn't a sympathy petition. I just wanted to explain why I am…why I *was* the way I was.'

She gave a small enlightened smile. 'You don't need to explain it to me. You closed yourself off to protect yourself from being hurt.'

He gave a harsh laugh. 'There's closing yourself off and there's doing what I did. I left Ekow to take up the mantle that should've been mine—my responsibility. I did to him the same thing my father did to me, and I didn't see my family for years because I was angry and ashamed. Then, when I came back, it was only so I could help my father perpetuate a feud that should never have started in the first place. You were right. What happened to Fiifi and Esi was a tragedy—that's all. It wasn't worth breaking up our families into even smaller pieces.'

She gave another short soft gasp. 'What are you saying?'

'That at some point I should've tried to be a better version of the man who sired me. Instead, I walked in his footsteps, uncaring of who I hurt.'

She shook her head, her look fierce as she glared at him. 'Don't say that about yourself. I refuse to believe that the man I gave myself to is the man you describe. You could've taken this place from me months ago, but you didn't. Did you authorise your brother to call in the bank loan?'

Anger roared through him again at what his father had done. 'No. I'd never do that. Bankers who take advantage of people in situations like yours are the worst of the worst.'

Her anger receded and a resigned smile appeared. 'Your father did that, didn't he?'

He nodded. 'He had our lawyers draw up papers to buy out the loan and file the demand. He waited until we were out of the country to do it. Ekow tried to stop him when he found out, but it was too late.'

Her gaze flitted over his face, then veered

away again. 'Is that why you're here? To discuss the resort?'

Another harsh laugh erupted from his tight throat. 'The resort is the last thing on my mind, Amelie.'

'Then why are you here?'

'I told you. I'm here for you.'

Her nostrils flared. 'But I'm not yours.'

'Believe me, I know. But I want you to be.'

Her eyes widened. 'What?'

'You heard me.'

Her face shuttered. 'But…you don't believe in love.'

He snorted. 'This is another revelation I'm grappling with. It turns out it doesn't matter how tightly you close yourself off. All it takes is a beautiful, compassionate woman with unstoppable determination and ferocious passion to sneak beneath your guard.'

'Atu…'

He jerked forward. 'I love you, Amelie. I may have loftily declared that love doesn't exist, but I have no other description for this feeling in my heart that I have for you and only you. I used my parents' marriage and what I saw of Fiifi and Esi's relationship as a yardstick to judge the world by. I never wanted anything like that, so I wrote off all relationships. But you made me want more, Amelie. You made me yearn for something more than landing the next deal. Waking up next to you made me realise what I was missing. The simple pleasure of holding your hand while you laughed brought me untold joy.'

Like magnets, his eyes were drawn to her belly again.

'I want to be a better father to our baby than mine was to me. And if we're blessed with more children, we will do even better…spread that love so none of them ever feel rejected.'

He wasn't aware he was drawing close until she tilted her face up to his, tears in her eyes. He brushed them away with his thumbs, his heart spilling over and burning through the desolation. The fact that she wasn't walking away made him hope that perhaps he had a chance.

'I'll do anything for a chance to show you that I can be different. Be a man you can be proud of.'

'You already are.'

His heart crashed into his ribs. 'Does that…? Are you…?'

Joy surged through his veins as she reached for his hand, lifted it and pressed it to her cheek. 'I've loved you since I was eighteen, Atu. I convinced myself it was just a teenage crush, that I wasn't worthy of you…'

He opened his mouth to quickly refute that, but she pressed a finger against his lips.

'Seeing you again made me recognise that it had been love all along…that I've been waiting for you all this time. But when you told me in Malaysia that you didn't believe in love, I lost hope. I convinced myself that simply being with you until we had to part was okay. Then I found out I was pregnant.'

Shame clouded over his hope and joy, and he grimaced. 'I know the statistics surrounding safe sex. I also recall how desperate we were for each other. That kind of desperation doesn't always lend itself to practising safe sex. And yet the news still floored me. And I let every moment of doubt about my ability to sustain a relationship ruin that moment. Please know that I wasn't rejecting you, my love. I was rejecting even the slightest possibility that I could be a good father to our baby.'

'Do you still doubt yourself?'

'I know that with you by my side I can be different. I'll do everything in my power to ensure that our child has a safe and happy home. That he or she will never feel the rejection and indifference I felt.'

'I know you will.'

He looked deeper into her eyes, joy surging anew at the look on her face. 'Does that mean…? Will you…?'

She nodded, tears flowing freely down her face. 'I love you, Atu. My deepest wish from the moment we met was to be with you.'

With a gruff exhalation that he would deny for ever was actually a half-sob, he gathered her into his arms. Pure happiness washed over his senses, and the dark hopelessness that had dogged him for the last two months vanished as he sealed his mouth to hers, stealing the kiss he'd been yearning for since she'd appeared.

When they finally broke apart, he cupped her jaw, his thumbs drifting reverently over her swollen lips.

'I want to get our mothers together. I don't care if they can't bear to be in the same room with each other. This is too important. I want to put a ring on your finger at the earliest opportunity. I want you walking down the aisle blooming with our baby. I need to make you mine as soon as possible, and then I want us to live the rest of our lives in sublime happiness.'

Sweet laughter exploded from her, her hands going around his waist to hold him as tightly as he was holding her. They kissed again, and when he lifted his head, her smile was pure bliss, a wonderful precursor to everything he knew he would achieve if she became his.

'Can we make that happen as soon as possible?' he asked.

'Oh, yes, I'll make it happen.'

His smile felt as if it would crack wide open with the happiness in his heart. 'Thank you.'

'Prepare yourself, though. My mother has been waiting for you to turn up for the last two months. She may have cursed your name a few times for your tardiness in claiming me and your child.'

He gathered her closer still, unable to bear even an inch of space between them. 'I'll make it up to her. I'll make it up to everyone. Now that I'm the head of the Quayson clan, I declare this senseless feud over.'

She smiled. 'Just like that?'

'You've shown me that with love underpinning what matters, anything is possible. I intend that to be my life's motto.'

Her tears flowed again. But he wasn't worried because he knew they flowed with love. For him. For the two families they were about to reshape into one, and for the brand-new family they would create.

Love would take care of them all.

And he couldn't wait to get started with her by his side.

EPILOGUE

Two years later

'I THOUGHT WE agreed that you wouldn't ride these things on your own?'

Amelie curbed a smile as she brought the electric buggy to a stop next to her glowering husband. But beneath the glower she spotted a flash of concern, and immediately forgave him for being all alpha.

'No, Husband. *You* decreed that I shouldn't ride them without you.'

He passed a hand over his nape, his nostrils pinching as he inhaled long and slow, and she swallowed the laugh bubbling up her throat.

'Amelie, you're eight months pregnant. Be reasonable.'

'If you didn't want me riding them, you shouldn't have introduced them to the resort. I suggested bicycles, remember?'

If anything, he looked even more pained. 'I shudder to think of you riding a bicycle while heavily pregnant with my baby.'

He helped her out of the buggy and she wrapped her arms around his neck, sighing in happiness when his hand slid possessively over her swollen stomach before snaking down to rest on her hips. She revelled in his warmth, his closeness, in the devotion that blazed from his eyes.

Her resort...*their* resort...was now three times the size of the original, even while they'd kept it exclusive and self-sustainable, and it made walking around it in her condition uncomfortable. Plus, she'd been testing out the snazzy new solar-powered buggies they were hoping to encourage their guests to use to explore the resort.

The project had taken a year to complete, and while their guests might not have a rainforest or sky-high trees to abseil down, they had the rich heritage of Fante history in nearby Cape Coast and Elmina, and her fishing tours and local sustainable jewellery workshops had been a hit.

Bookings had gone through the roof, and the announcement of her new role as Vice President of the Quayson Group had been met with sound approval.

But, while she was thrilled that the career she'd always dreamed of was now in full realisation, it was her personal life that fulfilled her the most.

'If you're done with attempting to give me a heart attack, can I tempt you with—?' He stopped as the sound of laughter pealed down the path, followed by a child's joyful squeal.

They turned to see her mother and his strolling towards them, each holding the chubby hand of their eighteen-month-old daughter, Amaya.

'Mama! Dada!'

Atu released Amelie and scooped up their daughter in his arms, making her squeal even louder. 'How's my gorgeous princess?'

Amaya beamed at her father, then immediately pointed at the buggy. 'Buggy! Ride!'

Atu groaned, a pained grimace crossing his face. 'See what you've done?' he asked from the corner of his mouth.

Amelie couldn't stop herself laughing.

His grimace melted away as he watched her, his eyes turning molten with love and the type of passionate heat that dismissed even the remotest idea that he found her ungainly form anything but intensely sexy.

'I can't help it if my daughter shares my adventurous spirit.'

The baby in her womb kicked, as if reminding them not to forget him. She passed her hand over her swollen belly, the love she'd thought she'd never have overflowing in her heart.

Atu moved closer, sliding his hand over hers.

The baby kicked again, and a wave of love moved over his face. 'I can't wait for our son to be here. He'll save me from being vanquished by feisty women.'

She snorted. 'Says the man who led the knocking ceremony instead of staying out of sight like tradition dictates. I didn't see you shying away from incurring the wrath of the elders.'

Usually only the leading members of both families conducted the knocking ceremony, the 'knocking' being a formal seeking of permission to take a woman's hand in marriage. But Atu had led his family, his impatience and the residual fear of rejection that hadn't quite died with his father pushing him to flout tradition.

He shrugged. 'I wasn't about to let anything stand in the way of my marrying you. I'd waited for you long enough,' he murmured, sliding one arm around her shoulders to draw her close.

She would have thought it impossible a moment ago, but she felt her heart grow even larger, happy tears threatening.

'We were just taking this one to lunch,' Naana Quayson said, her indulgent smile encompassing them both.

No longer under his father's overbearing influence, his mother had gained a second lease of life—which included utterly doting on her grand-daughter. She'd thrown herself into planning their wedding, much to their secret frustration sometimes, and was now co-opting her own mother into organising an elaborate christening celebration for her second child, in between feverish attempts to find a bride for Ekow.

She saw a figure moving towards them from the beach and smiled. Ekow had driven to Saltpond for the weekend. He was a frequent visitor when she, Atu and his niece weren't travelling to their other resorts.

The resemblance between the brothers was striking. They both had the same jaw-dropping presence and bone structure, although Ekow's eyes were a shade lighter than Atu's, and Amelie found his smile wasn't quite as breath-robbing as his brother's.

She caught the frown pleating his eyebrows as he got closer. 'Is everything okay?' she asked.

Ekow's jaw clenched before he neutralised his features as his niece peered up at him. He stroked a finger down her soft cheek, then tickled her under her chin. Once he'd earned himself a giggle, he answered. 'I've been dealing with an online security issue at the bank. Every time I think it's handled, it rears its head again.'

'It's not like you to be annoyed over a simple IT problem,' Atu said.

Ekow's nostrils flared in annoyance. 'It is when it's been going on for several weeks.'

Atu frowned. 'So it's not a simple tech issue?'

Ekow grunted. 'My cybersecurity team is handling it. Their preliminary report has pinpointed the source to South Africa. I might need to head down there and deal with whoever's attempting to hack into my bank...'

Since getting reacquainted with her husband's family, Amelie had learned that the streak of ruthlessness his father had engendered in them ran deep. With Atu, it had been the cloak he'd used to hide the hurt of his father's indifference and rejection.

Seeing the look in Ekow's eyes now, she wondered how deep his wounds ran. He caught her gaze and the look mellowed, that trademark devastating Quayson smile sliding into place. 'For now, though, I'm going to immerse myself in the delights of this awesome place.'

He sauntered off with his niece and the two grandmothers.

'Your brother has that look in his eyes you used to get when you were in warrior mode,' she said.

Atu smiled. 'I won my queen. I no longer need

that particular setting. Now I'm more about making love. Repeatedly…' he growled in her ear.

'Well, I pity whoever is messing with his beloved bank.'

'So do I. But enough about my brother…' He took her hand and helped her back into the buggy.

'Where are we going?'

'Somewhere we won't be disturbed for at least an hour. Unless anyone wants me back in warrior mode,' he promised darkly, making her laugh again.

A few minutes later Amelie gasped at the sight before her. A bountiful picnic had been laid out, complete with large throw pillows for her to rest on.

'You've brought me to my favourite place.'

It was the spot where he'd told her he loved her. The place where the miracle of love had come true for them.

'Of course. I had to get you alone somehow.'

'You get me to yourself every single night.'

He gave a smug smile, which slowly turned molten as he took her hand and helped her onto the blanket.

'Even if I could spend every second of every day with you, it wouldn't be enough. I intend to love and treasure you through this life and well into however many afterlives we get.'

Tears prickled her eyes. 'I promise to do the same,' she vowed.

* * * * *